TALL TALES
OF
MALAYSIA

JAMES M. BOURKE

authorHOUSE®

AuthorHouse™ UK
1663 Liberty Drive
Bloomington, IN 47403 USA
www.authorhouse.co.uk
Phone: UK TFN: 0800 0148641 (Toll Free inside the UK)
UK Local: (02) 0369 56322 (+44 20 3695 6322 from outside the UK)

This is a work of fiction. Names, characters and incidents in these stories are the product of the author's imagination. Any reference to actual persons, living or dead, is purely coincidental.

Published by AuthorHouse 03/17/2022

ISBN: 978-1-6655-9762-3 (sc)
ISBN: 978-1-6655-9763-0 (e)

Print information available on the last page.

This book is printed on acid-free paper.

INTRODUCTION

Tall Tales of Malaysia is a collection of 18 short stories about life in the multi-ethnic Federation of Malaysia where the writer lived for several years. Many famous writers, such as Joseph Conrad, Anthony Burgess and W. Somerset Maugham have left us haunting tales from the steaming jungles of Malaysia and a graphic account of the grace and beauty of that exotic land and the enduring charm of the friendliest people in Southeast Asia.

Writers of fiction always looks for odd events and eccentric people to make their narrative interesting. Hence, the focus in most of the stories is on the follies and foibles, fears and frustrations, conflicts and concerns among the different races that one finds in a multi-racial, multicultural society. Each story is a window on a fascinating aspect of Malaysian life and the several diverse races that live there-the Malays, the Chinese, the Indians, the Orang Asli and the indigenous people of Borneo. Malaysia is a rich tapestry of many different colours, which added to the natural beauty of the country and a warm languid climate make it a Paradise on earth or so one might imagine.

The book is more than a collection of short stories. It is a collage of cultural, social and political commentary. Each story has a distinctive Malaysian flavor, be it 'hantu' (spirits), life on the plantations, bomohs and djinns, snakes and tigers, the original people-the Orang Asli and the indigenous people of Sabah and Sarawak. Everywhere you go in Malaysia, you hear incredible stories about the clash of cultures, gargantuan scandals and bitter political strife but you have to remember that only 50% of what you hear has any basis in truth. The stories, though fictional, capture the tormented soul of the nation. Are the stories true? Now, that's a silly question. Everybody knows that story-telling in Malaysia is based on the understanding that truth must never get in the way of a good story.

The short story genre has been much used in colonial times by great writers such as Somerset Maugham and others. Today many Malaysians are writing in English, even though their mother tongue may be Malay, Chinese, or Tamil. A brief postscript lists some of the writers that have made a significant contribution to the large corpus of creative writing in English that has emerged in Malaysia.

For the benefit of those unfamiliar with Malay words used a few endnotes are provided after each story. Malaysian English contains a lot of words transferred from Malay and Chinese.

James M Bourke
Dublin
17th March, 2022.

Contents

THE UNWANTED WIFE

From the balcony of his studio in Jalan Lintas, Nelson Dampian gazed out over the sacred mountain, Aki Nabalu,[1] a majestic sight in the morning light. He had painted its stunning peaks from many different angles and he had somehow managed to capture not only its vibrant colours and its many textures but also its mystique. Nelson was very much a Kadazan[2] artist. He painted their villages, their bamboo dwellings, men and women in traditional dress, padi fields, upland valleys, their markets, black buffaloes and scenes from the Harvest Festival.

Nelson's father, Jacob, was a barber in Donggongon, a small town in Penampang, about ten kilometers south of Kota Kinabalu. It is a special place in Kadazan culture, overlooked by Aki Nabalu, the sacred mountain, home to the undead. There, many spirits dwell among the bare rocks, in the tall grasses, in the thickets and montane scrub. The mountain and had a profound effect on the young Nelson. It was home to many 'hantu'.[3]

Nelson received a good education at La Salle College in Tanjung Aru. It was there that his artistic talent was nurtured by the art teacher, Brother Julian. It was clear to everyone that Nelson was a boy of exceptional artistic talent. Fortunately for Nelson, Brother Julian managed to obtain a bursary for him to study art at La Salle College of the Arts in Singapore. At that time, in 1986, the college was located at St. Patrick's College on the East Coast Road. Even though it had only a small student population, it was already gaining recognition as the foremost art institution in the region, offering diploma and degree courses in Design and Fine Art, under the guidance of its famous founder, Brother McNally. The focus in all its courses was creativity. Its mission was to give art students the confidence and space to be what they wanted to be, to develop their individual vision and style. Nelson would admit that the best three years of his life were spent at La Salle. Besides, he loved the enchanting city of Singapore most of all because it was there, he met his future wife. She was not a Singapore girl but a beautiful Chinese girl from a small town in Malacca.

Her name was Wendy Lim. Her given name was Hong but outside of the family she was known as Wendy. Many children of Hokkien origin speak English outside the home and adopt an English name. She came from Merlimau, a small town in the State of Malacca. Like many small towns in Malaysia, it was a rather dull place with little architectural appeal, just shop houses with rusted corrugated iron roofs, cafes and a central market. The town was surrounded by clusters of colourful traditional houses and six kilometers south of the town were the mangrove swamps along the Sungai Kesang. Life in Merlimau was as dead as the proverbial dodo. Not surprisingly, many young people drifted to the big cities – Malacca, Johor Bahru and Singapore.

Wendy's father, Ng Poh Lim, was a man of sober habits and much wisdom. He was known locally as Doc Lim. He was the embodiment of the ideal gentleman as defined in the analects of Confucius. For him, the goal of living was the cultivation of wisdom. Nothing else mattered. He specialised in traditional Chinese medicine and his shop in Jalan Meru contained potions, ointments, oils and herbal medicines for every conceivable illness. The local people had absolute confidence in Doc Lim's diagnosis and treatment. His shop was a busy place and both his wife Gina and daughter Wendy served behind the counter. Although Christian, Wendy was brought up in a household imbued with ancient Chinese lore. Tai Chi was performed every morning and on the Feast of the Hungry Ghosts, joss-sticks were lit. As in Malay culture, there was a profound respect for the departed. By the time Wendy had completed her secondary education, she had acquired a good knowledge of Materia Medica[4] and the theory of medicine as expounded in the 'Yellow Emperor's Inner Canon'.[5] Nobody was surprised when in 1986, she decided to study medicine at the College of Traditional Chinese Medicine in Singapore.

Wendy found life in Singapore much to her liking. The only problem was money. Singapore is an expensive place, especially for a young woman on a tight budget. College students are always eager to earn a little money, serving in bars and cafes in their free time. Wendy replied to an advertisement for a part-time artists' model at La Salle and she was offered two afternoon sessions each week. She was sketched and painted from different angles by several students including Nelson. It was not long before he became bewitched by his subject. Wendy was a beautiful woman. She was tall, slim and very athletic looking. Nelson marvelled at the sheer perfection of this goddess, at her clear skin, her raven black hair tied in a long ponytail, her arms smooth as alabaster, her gentle curves, her slender waist and sinuous legs that a ballerina would have envied. Not for the first time in the history of art, did the painter fall in love with his subject. At first, it was a slow burning love that dare not speak its name. Wendy was mesmerised and terrified at the same time. It all happened so suddenly, so unexpectedly. But there was no escape from all-encompassing love. Wendy and Nelson were smitten. They agreed that, upon graduation, they would marry and embark on married life in Kota Kinabalu.

Nelson returned to Kota Kinabalu at the end of 1989. His family and friends were delighted with his progress and they helped him set up a small studio in Jalan Lintas. He rented a space in the art gallery in the Cultural Centre and he appointed his cousin Marcus as his agent. His early paintings were of familiar sights – Mount Kinabalu, the padi fields, the harbour, the Clock Tower, traditional Kadazan dwellings, hornbills and oxen. They were bright, vibrant and very different from the style of traditional landscapes. Nelson was not afraid to mix different colours in novel ways, for instance, red and tangerine, vermillion and gold, ultramarine and indigo. His art blossomed as he gradually discovered the properties of light and colour, topographical accuracy, portraiture and the use of symbolism and mythology. In Singapore, most of his painting was done indoors. Back in Kota Kinabalu, like Monet and Cezanne, he preferred to paint en plein air. He made his own paints by grinding pigment powders with linseed oil. He believed that while he was painting, he was capturing a moment in time. Each stroke on the canvas had to say something about the object, the air, the light and the atmosphere. Each painting had to reflect a profound depth of feeling and his inner vison. He believed that art can change your life. It can transcend life, just like music or poetry. When you saw a Nelson painting in the National Gallery, it stood out and by some magical power, sucked you in. It touched something deep inside you and you were unable to say what it was. His early work especially displayed images of the brightest colours – butterflies, snakes, exotic birds – as well as somber and ominous skies, scudding clouds, mountain peaks and raging sea.

Wendy graduated the following year and having obtained the approval and blessing of their respective parents, she and Nelson got engaged. The wedding followed in due course. It was a memorable and magnificent ceremony attended by family and friends from Malacca and Sabah. It was, everyone agreed, a marriage made in Heaven. Weddings in Sabah are elaborate affairs and extend over a week of feasting and traditional ritual. Large quantities of lihing (rice wine) are consumed and stuffed pigs are roasted on a spit. Gongs announce the glad tidings far and wide and guests let down their hair and engage in joyous traditional singing and dancing.

For several years after their wedding, Nelson and Wendy knew only married bliss. They both prospered in their chosen professions. Nelson continued to produce and sell superb paintings to Sabah's nouveau riche. Wendy also enjoyed instant success. She opened her own clinic in Jalan Gaya – the 'Kita Clinic of Holistic Medicine'. Before long, she had more patients than she could cope with and although she charged only modest fees, she soon became very rich. However, like many rich Chinese ladies in Malaysia, she liked to play mahjong. In fact, she became addicted to the game and played it several times a week. Chinese ladies do not play mahjong for buttons; they play for large stakes. As in all gambling ventures, players often lose large amounts of money. Nelson had no idea that his wife had become a big gambler until he found that substantial sums of money had disappeared from their joint bank account. She had squandered a fortune trying to cover her losses at mahjong. Furthermore, she had pawned some of his best paintings. Nelson was not amused nor was he satisfied with her explanation. She told him that she was charmed into surrendering all their money after inadvertently touching a magic stone by their Indonesian amah who was skilled in the black art. He was furious and distraught at his wife's foolishness. He spent days brooding over his misfortune, which left him emotionally traumatised. In the end, he decided to banish Wendy from his house and his life.

'Go away from here and do not come back. Our marriage is over!' he announced in chilling tones. Without a word of protest, Wendy packed a few of her belongings in a rucksack and walked away, unsure where she might end up.

Nelson assumed that Wendy would return the next day but she did not. Then, when his rage had subsided, he organised a search party and they combed the entire area but found nothing. His wife had disappeared without a trace. He returned home full of remorse for having acted precipitously. Then, almost three weeks later, he received shocking news. The Mountain Rescue team had been patrolling the lower slopes of Mount Kinabalu and there, in a deep ravine, they found the partly decayed body of a woman. It was impossible to say whether she had fallen to her death or been murdered. They took the decomposed body to be Nelson's wife and had it transported to his house in Kota Kinabalu. The poor man was beside himself with grief and shame. He fell down and cried uncontrollably. In his Kadazan mind, Aki Nabalu had punished him for his grave wrong. The body of the dead woman was cremated and her ashes deposited in an urn in Nelson's studio. He was consoled, to some extent, to be re-united with his departed wife. She was no longer physically present but she was present in his heart and in the urn.

In fact, Wendy had not gone to Mount Kinabalu. She went straight to the Central Station and caught the express bus to Sandakan, on the other side of Sabah. There, she was directed to the Good Shepherd Home, a charitable institution for fallen women and women in distress. It was run by the Sisters of Charity. The matron, Sister Magdalene, listened to her story and appointed her as medical officer to the other inmates, on a modest stipend. It was not what Wendy really wanted. Her plan was to return home to Nelson as soon as she received appropriate therapy. Sr. Magdalen was skilled in addiction therapy and it was agreed that Wendy should return home as soon as she had overcome her addiction to gambling.

And so, after spending six weeks at the Good Shepherd Home, Wendy returned to Kota Kinabalu. She arrived at Nelson's house at midnight and knocked on the door. Not knowing who was there, he called out: "Who is it?" Wendy answered: "It is me, your loving wife. Open the door." However, Nelson was convinced that the sweet voice at his door was not that of his wife but the dreaded Pontianak, the blood-sucking vampire, seeking a male victim. He bolted the door and sprinkled the doorpost with holy water.

'Go away, you evil one!' he shouted, 'My wife is here with me.' Wendy knew that Nelson would never allow her to return and she began walking towards the sacred mountain, Aki Nabalu. What else would a homeless woman in Sabah do?

ENDNOTES:

1 *Aki Nabalu:* Mount Kinabalu, the sacred mountain overlooking Kota Kinabalu, Sabah. Meaning: 'the revered place of the dead.'

2 *Kadazan*: The largest indigenous ethnic group in the state of Sabah, Borneo. Also called Dusun or Kadazan Dusun. See Tamara Thiessen (2016*). Borneo: Sabah Sarawak Brunei.* 3rd.ed. UK: Bradt Travel Guides.

3 *hantu*: ghosts, the undead

4 '*Materia Medica*': A Latin text on medical matters, including herbalism; natural healing materials and their properties.

5 '*Yellow Emperor's Inner Canon*': An ancient Chinese medical text compiled over 2,200 years ago.

INTO THE HEART OF BORNEO

I always looked forward to visiting Sarawak which I used to do frequently when I lived in Brunei. Every weekend there would be a mass exodus of expatriates to the border at Kuala Lura. The only commodity on sale in that ramshackle border post was alcohol. Bruneian residents parked their cars on the Brunei side of the disputed border and walked across no-man's-land to Linghi's bar and bottle store, the most popular of several watering holes on the Malaysian side of the border. Linghi is a jolly little Iban man who sells alcohol at duty free prices, shipped over from the island of Labuan. There are no licensed premises at the border and Linghi ducks and weaves to stay in a lucrative business which is controlled by the Chinese Triads.

Some people would take their cars across and then drive all the way to Limbang town and possibly spend a night at the Royal Park Hotel. You had to be careful where you parked your car because they were known to disappear and never be seen again. At that time, Limbang had something of a reputation as a 'cowboy town' offering easy access to wine, women and song. It was a quiet town at that time, a little like Corleone in Sicily, run by the Mafia. The Chinese mafia were said to have a variation on the Mafia's 'cement shoes'-the body was weighed with rocks and tied to a large log which was then floated down the river. The crocodiles did the rest.

During school holidays, people tended to drive to Miri or fly to Kuching, both very attractive holiday destinations. Old hands, however, would avoid the 'Miri madness' like the plague and instead fly to Kuching and enjoy five-star comfort at the Kuching Hilton. However, the problem with staying in a hotel, in the lap of luxury, is that one misses out on the excitement of real adventure by venturing into the interior, into the land of the hornbill, mighty rivers, enchanting rainforest and contact with some of the many ethnic groups that live on their traditional lands in longhouses, far from the towns and cities. To reach these communal settlements, you travel by longboat up muddy rivers and those kind 'ulu'[1] people would greet you like a long lost relative, share their food with you, perform native dances and make jolly with home-made tuak.[2] Urban life did not appeal to those forest dwellers. They lived off the bounty of the rainforest and the waterways and grew their own food. Their needs were simple. Their food was organic and all they needed to buy was salt and cooking oil. Everything else was grown or obtained from Mother Nature.

Even though I have not myself journeyed into the heart of Sarawak, I met a man who has. His name is Ross Hamilton. He came originally from London but he spent many years working for the Brunei government as a legal adviser. He lived in some style in a salubrious condominium called Ong Sung Ping near Prince Jefri's unfinished palace. I first met him at the Civil Service club in Kota Batu. We used to play the odd game of tennis and even though he was 60, I could never beat him as he played with power, precision and top spin. I got to know Ross quite well over another game, chess. We would play once a week, at his place or mine and once again I was no match for the grand master. However, he seemed to enjoy our weekly game and after a few glasses of whisky, he would drop his natural reserve and share all the latest gossip and scandals, of which there were plenty. He was a living encyclopedia on all aspects of life in Borneo, with a special interest in its rich and varied bird life. He had read all the great books on Borneo-Conrad, Maugham, Burgess and Buck. He was a great admirer of Conrad's eastern novels *Almayer's Folly*[3], *Lord Jim* and *An Outcast of the Islands*. He had over a hundred Borneo-inspired novels in his study and I was allowed to borrow them.

Ross had a Chinese housekeeper or mistress called Heng Gee. Her mission in life was to mind her man, who had a heart condition and was not supposed to drink or smoke. However, Ross loved a glass of malt whisky and he used to be a heavy smoker. However, his diligent minder kept the drinks cabinet under lock and key and opened it only when there was a guest. Since she also smoked, she allowed Ross to smoke five cigarettes a day and they were duly placed in his silver cigarette case each evening. He was rather proud of his silver cigarette case which he told me was the only gift he had ever bought for himself. He bought it in London on his 50th birthday because he felt he deserved it, having spent a lifetime working overseas in the Middle East and Southeast Asia. Heng Gee also supervised his diet, paid his bills and managed his affairs. It was curious to see a kindly English gentleman so utterly henpecked. For instance, Ross would say to Heng Gee: 'I think James would like a wee dram.' And the unsmiling Heng Gee would respond: 'Would he now?' in her most sarcastic tone of voice. Soon, a silver tray would appear with a bottle of Chevas Regal, two tumblers and an ice bucket. But all of that is by the way.

One evening, Ross gave me a blow-by-blow account of a journey he had made into the heart of Sarawak. It was as good a presentation as I have ever attended. Like a good teacher, whenever he mentioned a specific place or event, he nailed it down with a visual or an object. He was not only a captivating speaker and raconteur but he was also an accomplished photographer. He punctuated his talk with magnificent colour transparencies and photographs mounted in an album. He explained that this trip had two objectives. Firstly, he was hoping to locate Conrad's settlement and trading post Sambir[4] which is mentioned in both *Almayer's Folly* and *An Outcast of the Island*. He knew was it was somewhere up a river in the south west of the country, its exact location known only to Captain Lingard. Secondly, as a dedicated bird-watcher, he was hoping to spot and photograph several different species of hornbill.[5]

He set out in the late afternoon and travelled to Kuala Belait on his ancient BSA motorcycle, looking like a bearded New Age traveller. He spent the first night in the government rest house there so as to be up bright and early to catch the car ferry across the Belait River. There was a bridge across the river but for some mysterious reason it could not be used as it had not been officially opened so people waited for hours to get across on the car ferry. Perhaps the Sultan of Brunei did not want his borders to be too porous for security reasons. Ross arrived at the ferry point at 6 a.m. to avoid the build-up of Miri-bound vehicles. Even so, there were twenty or more vehicles before him. Then he headed for Miri where he rested, did some shopping and spent most of the day in the nearby Lambir Hills National Park, famous for its dense dipterocarp trees and its abundant wildlife. However, his focus was exclusively on the vast population of birds nesting or feeding there, including several species of hornbill. He spent the night in one of the cheaper inns, the Plaza Regency on Jalan Brooke. Next morning, he was up at daybreak and after a substantial Malay breakfast, he set out on a long ride along the Trans-Borneo Highway to Bintulu. The highway was quite busy and he had little time to admire the scenic countryside as he passed padi fields, palm oil and pepper plantations and dense forests. He was exhausted by the time he reached Bintulu.

Bintulu had little of interest to offer Ross. He checked into a budget hotel with a view across the Kemena River. However, the town had something he would not miss – the Wildlife Park. It is one of the few places where you can see a variety of birds – hornbills by the dozen, storks, eagles and cheeky mynah birds. There are also a few orangutans, gibbons and Malaysian tigers. Ross was quite pleased to encounter and photograph a pair of Black hornbills which seemed to be playing hide-and-seek with each other among the sago palms. He asked a park attendant if there were many hornbills in the wetlands. His reply surprised him: 'Yes, too many. They hide in the sago palms and prey on small birds and insects. So unfair, lah.' Nobody he met seemed to have heard of Conrad or Almayer or Captain Lingard, so it seemed unlikely that 'Sambir', if it existed at all, was anywhere in or near the boomtown of Bintulu.

Ross's next destination was Dalat but he stopped for a brief visit to Mukah, ancestral home of the Melanau people. On the way, he passed countless wooden bridges in the 'land of a thousand rivers'. The big industry in Mukah is the harvesting of the sago palm and its working into sago flour which is exported to Japan, Singapore and the UK. The waterfront was a hive of activity, being both a fish market and a ferry terminal. All travel in the area is by boat and fishing is a way of life. Ross went on a brief tour of the vast sago swamp, past old wooden houses sitting precariously on the banks of the peat-black river and below them, platforms where the sago was worked. On every side, he noticed smiling faces, open-air food stalls, ox carts laden with pineapples, banana trees and in the durian trees beyond the rivers, several pairs of Bushy-crested hornbills. For Ross, it was a magic land of smiling faces, hornbills and the sweetest pineapples on the planet.

It was late in the afternoon when he reached the tiny hamlet of Dalat. It is mentioned by Christopher H. Gallop [6] in his account of his journeys across Sabah and Sarawak. It is not mentioned in Conrad's first novel 'Almayer's Folly' but some people have speculated that Dalat might have been Captain Lingard's famous trading post Sambir. It had several similarities to Conrad's description. There was a river, the Batang Oya, fringed with coconut palms and there were wooden houses nestled along both banks of the river. Furthermore, it was conveniently situated just off the Bintulu-Sibu highway, which in those days was no more than a dirt track. Ross decided to follow Gallop's advice: 'When in Dalat, stay at the Hoover.' The Dalat Hoover is not a five-star hotel; it is a no-star hotel. He was given the front room on the upper storey. Even though it was more like a shack than a hotel, it was a friendly place, run by two elderly Foochow ladies. One could not complain about the room rate which was RM10 per night. The only problem was that there was non-stop karaoke music surging up from the bar below. However, the food was first class. Ross feasted on ikan merah[7] and udang.[8] However, from his conversation with the Foochow ladies, he concluded that Dalat was not Sambir after all. Firstly, if it was, it would have been known by the local people but nobody there had ever heard of Sambir or Conrad. Secondly, Sambir was a large trading post but there was no evidence of such in Dalat. Finally, Dalat was too close to the sea to be a safe haven for a secret trading post. The Sea Dayaks were pirates and they would have found it.

Ross decided to leave his motorcycle at the Hoover Hotel as he moved inland since river transportation was both plentiful and cheap. Next day, he caught the 'Sri Bahagia' speedboat to Sibu. The three-hour journey cost a mere RM10. The boat cut a swathe through the Kut Channel and entered the broad Batang Igan to Sibu, which is the doorway to the mighty Rajang River, the longest river in Borneo.

Sibu is a busy port, where many a fierce battle was fought between warring tribes. It lies astride the Rajang River, with four separate wharfs for cargo and passengers going upriver or downriver. The lower reaches were populated by the Sea Dayaks and the upper reaches, beyond Belaga and the rapids, were the ancestral lands of the Orang Ulu or Land Dayaks. Ross stayed at the Kawan Hotel in Jalan Chengal. There he rested and caught up with events in the outside world in the *Straits Times*. The doorman at the hotel was an elderly Iban, Alex Ontong. He was something of a local historian and tour guide. He had heard of but not read *Almayer's Folly* and he was convinced that Sibu was Conrad's Sambir. In olden days, his parents had often mentioned a trading post, now a coal depot, on Arang Wharf which was said to be owned by an 'Orang Belanda' (Dutchman) who traded in spices, sago and rosewood. Perhaps the Dutchman was Almayer but one could not be sure.

Then Alex went on to talk about the good old days under the White Rajahs.[9] saying: 'Dem was good mans, the Rajah Brookes. We sorry when they leave. All people love them too much.' He had been employed as a tracker by the British during the Japanese occupation. 'Sibu was bombed during the war. Japanese show no mercy. Kill everyone like chickens.' Ross told Alex that his final destination was Kapit.[10] 'No problem', said Alex 'I fix travel and accommodation.' In Sarawak, everyone has a relative who will look after you. His nephew Joshua had a boat with an outboard engine and he used it to ferry up to 10 passengers to Kapit where they would be taken to Bundong Longhouse where they would enjoy Iban hospitality. Next morning, Ross and six intrepid German tourists made their way to Kapit Wharf where Joshua was waiting in his long boat. They boarded the narrow vessel and set off up the mighty Rajang River, an exhilarating experience. On the way, the Germans had great fun fishing. Joshua told them: 'Must catch plenty fish. No fish, no food.' They passed several huge crocodiles bobbing about like great logs in the muddy water. And every now and then, they noticed in the far distance, pairs of hornbills in free flight. The trip to Kapit took three hours.

Kapit is a one-horse town, with only one bank, a post office, rows of wooden shop-houses with corrugated iron roofs, open storm drains, a Catholic church, a Methodist church, a mosque and a Chinese temple. Once back on terra firma, Ross and his German fellow travellers had lunch at a hawker stall. The Germans decided to spend some time exploring the town but Ross and Joshua went straight to Bundong Longhouse because Ross was keen to explore the surrounding forest in his quest for hornbills. And he was not disappointed. His guide took him on a 10 km trail to the top of Bukit Lambir and the waterfall above the lake. They encountered gibbons, dusky leaf monkeys, macaques, flying lemurs, several species of snake, lizards and a host of birds both large and small including six of the eight known species of Borneo hornbill and a host of butterflies. The hornbills were making quite long flights from one patch of forest to another in their search for trees in fruit, their broad wings making a loud 'whoosh, whoosh' sound. The awesome sights, sounds and smells in this Garden of Eden blew one's mind away. Footsore and weary, Ross made his way back to the longhouse where he joined his German companions for dinner. They had a most pleasant meal and great fun because after several glasses of tuak, the Germans became jolly and joined in the Monkey Dance performed by the Ibans.

And so, Ross's great journey into the heart of Sarawak came to an end. The homeward trip took only three days. He returned to Sibu and Dalat where his motorcycle was waiting. Eventually, he crossed over the border into Brunei at Kuala Belait and made his way back to his comfortable home at Ong Sung Ping. He felt completely at home among the simple people of rural Sarawak. He admired their diligence and independence. They were the 'forgotten ones' and they received little support from the State government. Instead, they worked together as a close-knit community and developed their own economy and welfare system. Ross found that the 'ulu' people were preoccupied with their basic daily needs but at the same time they were interested in national issues such as good governance, equality, human rights and education. He discovered that many Dayaks were well-read and educated and their mindset was no longer that of food gatherer, head hunter and forest dweller. They were concerned at some of the developmental schemes launched by the Federal government, supposedly on their behalf. Their ancestral lands were slowly being confiscated. Logging companies had moved in, cleared much of the primary forest and replaced it with palm oil plantations. Consequently, many species of fauna and flora had disappeared due to loss of habitat. Clearly, the old synergy between the 'ulu' people and their environment was being put at risk.

For Ross, his journey into the heart of Sarawak was also a journey inside himself. He saw that there was another way to live in peace in harmony with one's environment. He admired and envied the stress-free natural lifestyle of the forest dwellers in the Garden of Eden. However, he dare not mention such an ungodly thought to his partner, Heng Gee. For her, the ulu people were uncivilized, indolent, still in the stone age; they were head-hunters who went about near naked in their hornbill head gear and blow pipes looking for deer, wild boar and monkeys to eat. They even feasted on monkey brains and other disgusting animal parts. Worst of all, they were spoilt rotten by Catholic and Methodist missionaries. Heng Gee's rant went on until Ross said: 'Yes, dear, now tell me what's for dinner?' Unlike Ross, she had no interest whatever in the many tribes and their age-old civilization that existed in the heart of Borneo.

ENDNOTES:

1   *ulu*: In Malay, the word means the interior of a country; in Singlish a remote place. The phrase *Orang Ulu* refers to upriver or interior people.

2   *tuak*: rice wine

3   *Almayer's Folly*, published in 1895, is Joseph Conrad's first novel. Kaspar Almayer is a young Dutch trader who is taken under the wing of the wily Captain Lingard. Almayer agrees to marry Lingard's adopted Malay child, hoping to inherit his wealth by running his trading post at Sambir in the Borneo jungle. Unfortunately, his many ventures constantly fail.

4   *Sambir*: The name of the Captain Lingard's remote and secret trading post which Ross failed to locate. Had he gone to Kuching, he would have discovered that Sambir is 15 km to the east of Kuching on the River Sabang. In *Lord Jim* he refers to another trading post at Patusan in Eastern Borneo.

5   *hornbill*: A large tropical bird having a large curved bill that typically has a large bony casque. Eight different species of hornbill have been identified in Borneo- the Rhinoceros, Oriental Pied, Wrinkled, Bushy-crested, Helmeted, Black, White-crowned and Wreathed Hornbill.

6   C. H. Gallop (2008). *Wanderer in Malaysian Borneo*. Subang: Marshall Cavendish.

7   *ikan merah:* Red snapper

8   *udang:* prawns

9   *White Rajahs*: The Brooke dynasty. See R. H. W. Reece (1982). *The Name of Brooke: The End of White Rajah Rule in Sarawak*. Kuala Lumpur: Oxford University Press.

10   *Kapit*: A small town 130 km from Sibu, in the interior of Borneo, accessible by speedboat up the Rajang River. It was founded by Charles Brooke in 1880 as a garrison town. Not much to see there apart from Fort Sylvia. Most of the ulu people in the Kapit area are Iban.

3

ACROSS SABAH ON
A MOTORBIKE

During my time in Brunei, I used to visit Labuan quite frequently. Among my many friends there was an English pipeline engineer with Murphy Oil. His name was Adam Turner. He came from Nottingham but he never wanted to return there. Still, he remained a devoted 'Forest'[1] fan and longed for the day that his team would return to the Premier League. He was a jolly character as was his wife, Salina binti Musa, a Malay lady of rare charm and beauty. I could see that Adam and Salina got along like a house on fire. He was something of a rough diamond, with a strong Northern accent but she was a graceful swan, educated by the nuns in Singapore. He was British; she was Malaysian. He was Christian; she was Muslim. He was funny and vulgar at times; she was always posh and elegant. I loved her way of summing up people and situations. I had always imagined that a posh Malay woman would never look at, much less marry, a foreigner. She laughed and said: 'We all belong to different races, religions, and traditions but we are all the same inside.' She was obviously a liberated woman, highly educated and a wonderful story teller. No visit to Labuan would be complete without a rendezvous with the Turners. We used to meet in one of the seafood restaurants, or in the Hilton lounge or in Ken's Irish bar.

Adam loved adventure and travel. He had a Kawasaki Ninja motorbike on which he explored the bye-ways and highways of Sabah and Sarawak. There is something very exciting and romantic about setting off on a powerful motorbike into the heart of Borneo. It was something I would have loved to have done in my younger years, enjoying the freedom of the open road and the magic of the rainforest. Adam's friends in Labuan thought it foolhardy of him to undertake such a hazardous journey alone and his good friend Haji Omar said 'only ghosts and evil spirits travel alone.' Adam conceded that Haji Omar had a point but it did not in an any way diminish his love of travel. One evening, over pints of Tiger beer, he gave me a blow-by-blow account of his great adventure-Sabah by bike.

Adam's plan was as follows. He would take the ferry to Lawas, spend a night there and early next morning ride from Lawas to Kota Kinabalu (KK) along the coastal road, a journey of some 150 km. On Day 2, he would cut across the northern shoulder of the Crocker Range on the road to Tambunan and then head north to Ranau and Kundasang. On Day 3, he'd ride all the way from Ranau across the belly of Sabah to Sandakan on the east coast. He hoped to visit some of the places associated with Agnes Keith, author of *Land Below the Wind*. Then, on Day 4, he'd head south to Lahad Datu. On Day 5, after visiting the remote Murut villages between the Kwamut and Kalabakang rivers, he hoped to reach Tawau on the Indonesian border. On Day 6, he planned to head north again over dirt tracks to the Danum Valley. On Day 7, all being well, he would make his way to the Maliau Basin, where he would overnight in a log cabin. Finally, on Day 8, he'd navigate his way across many rivers all the way back to Lawas, where his journey began.

I really envied Adam because Sabah is a magic land, an enormous country bigger than France; a land of stunning mountains, muddy rivers, dense rainforest, tea and palm-oil plantations; a land of diverse races-Kadazan, Dusum, Murut, Chinese and Malays; the land of empire builders; outpost of the British Empire; the country that once belonged to the British Chartered Company; the land that we discovered in the stories by Joseph Conrad, Somerset Maugham and Agnes Keith; the place where 'there ain't no Ten Commandments'. I had been to KK several times with my family and we climbed Mount Kinabalu. We had been to Kudat at the tip of Borneo, visited a Rungus longhouse and gazed upon the meeting of the waters-the Sulu Sea and the South China Sea. The crowning glory of Sabah is its rainforest. With over three million hectares of gazetted forest reserves, hundreds of endangered species are being preserved for the future-the orangutans, the wah wahs (gibbons), pigmy elephants, the

Bornean banteng (wild cattle) and a glittering array of snakes, birds, and butterflies. Sabah has it all but it also has some of the poorest people in the Federation of Malaysia.

One morning in May, Adam rode his bike down to the ferry terminal in Labuan and got himself and his bike on the ferry to Lawas. The ferry boat chugged its way across the choppy sea to the sleepy logging town of Lawas. It was Adam's first trip to that remote Sarawakian outpost. He checked into the Perdana Hotel, a clean well-run budget hotel but definitely not the Hilton. Adam liked the old-world feel of Lawas but there was little he could do there other than eat and drink. The cafes were full of chattering men, many in dungarees and boiler suits, enjoying a long lunch break over coffee or beer. He explored the town on his bike which was much admired by the locals. In the evening, the bars brightened up a little, with some loud music and a few comely maidens seeking company. Many of the older men just sat there in stony silence, or watched an appalling Bollywood movie on the television screen. The younger men played pool and everyone smoked. Adam wondered why anyone would want to live in such a remote and soulless place.

Next morning, he set off on the first leg of his grand tour of Sabah. The long ride to KK was pretty uneventful. The road was busy with heavily laden trucks heading for KK. Adam did not stop to admire the sea view. In any case, it is no longer a coastal road after Sipitang. His first stop was Beaufort, a quiet provincial town on the railway line to Tenom. The town consists of rather dilapidated wooden shophouses. It is on the leeward of the Crocker Range which dominates the western province from Sipitang to KK.

Then, on his bike again, Adam headed for KK which he reached by midday-at least that is what it said on the Atkinson Clock Tower at the foot of Signal Hill. He checked into the Pantai Inn, a clean well-run hotel in the KK Lama district. He could have stayed in one of the many luxury hotels along the waterfront but all he wanted after a hard day on the road was a good night's sleep. The hotel was a little frayed at the edges but the staff were most considerate and jolly. After lunch, he wandered about the city, which he knew quite well from previous visits. He had climbed Mt. Kinabalu previously, he had been to the islands and had stayed in the Promenade Hotel. This time, he wanted something different. He was keen to explore Sabah's rich history and heritage. He needed to find out more about the culture of the indigenous Kadazan, Dusun, Rungus and Murut people. He intended to talk to those people and see what they made of recent developments in Sabah and their relationship with the Federal government in KL. The following morning, spent some time in the Sabah Museum and the Heritage Village. Back at the hotel, he asked the ever-charming manageress, Marissa, where the best place to have dinner was. She named half a dozen superb seafood restaurants nearby but Adam had been to such places dozens of times back home in Labuan. He wanted something different. The kind lady then said if he wanted something really different, he should make his way to the Filipino Barbeque Centre behind the Filipino Market. She showed exactly where to find it on the map. Here there is no chef de cuisine on duty, no fancy menu-just several rows of long tables and an array of seafood that is stunning – chili crab, lobster, tuna collars, shrimp, squid, stingray and red snapper. Here you can feast on local cuisine at its finest but you will not find pork, stuffed frog, rat, snails or grubs which are considered non-halal. This particular market is run by Filipino Muslims. The food is served on banana leaf, together with a helping of rice and a selection of side dishes – chilly, bamboo shoots, water spinach stir-fried with shrimp paste, local wild fern, seaweed, and a choice of sauces. You eat with the hand, Malay style and there is a small basin of water for washing your hand. Adam loved the food and the caring attention of the Filipina waiters.

On his way back to his hotel, he stopped off at 'Cocoon', one of the many watering holes along the waterfront. Of course, in a KK bar you never drink alone. He was soon joined by the most gorgeous female in all God's creation. – an Indonesian goddess, tall, slim, with long jet-black hair, a face cut out of Carrara marble and eyes that shone like diamonds. Of course, it would be rude not to buy a lady a drink, even though she might be a sarong party girl. Adam was not looking for adventure of the romantic kind but who could resist the charms of such a ravishing houri?[3] Her name was Liliyana and she came from Tarakan in Indonesia. She said she was a club hostess, but Adam suspected that she really was a 'comfort woman' especially when she whispered in his ear: 'I love you long time.' They had a second drink, and a third, by which time Adam felt he had crossed the line. Fortunately, a wealthy Arab client wanted to chat up Liliyana and that was Adam's cue to escape.

To get to Sandakan from KK, you can choose the high road or the low road. The high road is the national expressway and the low road starts at Penampang and cuts across the upper shoulder of the Crocker Range on the way to Tambunan. Adam chose the latter and climbed up into the cool air of the mountain, passed the Rafflesea Reserve, where specimens of the world's largest flower can be found. He did not stop, however, nor did he visit Tambunan, but headed north again to Ranau. Below him was the wide expanse of the Pegalan Valley, Sabah's rice basket. Here, he was quite alone in what looked like a little bit of heaven. Below him lay the great valley that was once the stronghold of Tambunan's most famous son, Mat Salleh, a Sulu prince and great warrior who declared war on the Chartered Company [3] in 1895. Hence, today any troublemaker in Malaysia is known as a Mat Salleh. Adam was well aware of the colonial history and exploitation of North Borneo. He knew about the shady deals that had enabled the British Chartered Company to acquire Sabah from the Sultan of Sulu just as James Brooke,[4] the White Rajah, had persuaded the Sultan of Brunei to cede Sarawak to him in 1841. Those were extraordinary deals and extraordinary times and as a result both Sarawak and Sabah became British colonies and Brunei became a British protectorate.

Adam next headed for Ranau, a rather uninspiring town of concrete shop blocks-a stopping off point for travellers on their way to Kinabalu National Park or Poring Hot Springs. He decided to check in at the Rafflesea Inn in the centre of town. He had a light lunch after which he travelled some 15 km back towards KK to visit the village of Kundasang and the War Memorial. He had lost two of his uncles in the Battle of Borneo. It was here that hundreds of British and Anzac POWs died during the infamous Ranau death marches [5] in 1945.

Adam returned to his modest hotel in Ranau and had dinner at Restaurant Double Luck. Next morning after a substantial Malay breakfast he set off on the next leg of his journey to Sandakan,-a challenging ride of 200 km across the hot belly of Sabah. He passed several villages and stopped only to refuel. There was no way he was going to bypass the Sepilok Orangutan sanctuary. It is here that orphaned and injured orangutans are brought to be rehabilitated for return to the wild. His daughter, Karri, would never have forgiven him had he not stopped off at Sepilok to visit the red apes, our closest cousins. The orangutans are consummate acrobats and in spite of their considerable bulk can sail through the treetops with the greatest of ease. They are endearing creatures, everybody's favourite ape. They look at you with melancholy eyes as if they were aware that they had missed out somewhere on the evolutionary chain.

In Sandakan, Adam stayed at Hotel London, overlooking the harbour. He wanted to see only one thing in the city-the Agnes Keith house in Jalan Istana. A visit there is a trip back in time to colonial days when Sandakan was the capital of North Borneo. The villa in which the Keiths lived in the 1930s is really a museum which documents Sandakan in all its colonial splendour. The adjacent English Tea House is the perfect place to re-live the British colonial experience; there, you can have watercress sandwiches and real English tea. No writer captures the contrasting lifestyle of the colonizers and the colonized in North Borneo as does Agnes Keith. She also tells of the dreadful treatment meted out by the Japanese during World War 2. Adam loved her two great classics *Land Below the Wind,* and *Three Came Home.* It must have been sheer hell for an American lady to live under the strictures of the British colonial administration, having to kowtow to the Governor General, the Resident and the British elite. She had to suppress her natural American euphoria and appear 'distant', saying 'How do you do?' in a manner that suggested nonchalant superiority. One had to endure all the hardships of colonial life with fortitude and a stiff upper lip as well as the alien culture, the heat and humidity, the mosquitoes and cockroaches, the endless hassle with native servants, the ever unwelcome incursion of snakes and lizards, the muddy rivers full of crocodiles and leeches. My God, who would want to live in such a place?

From Sandakan, Adam thought it would be fun to follow in the footsteps of Agnes Keith and her husband Harry to Ulu Kwamut, the last outpost of the head-hunters. It is always exciting to venture into the great unknown where there are no shops, or cafes, or even roads, only 'mouse trails' through the jungle. He said goodbye to Hotel London and to the porter Amir whose last words rang in his ears: 'Go in peace and watch your head.'

Adam travelled due South to Sukau where he had lunch. Feeling refreshed, he headed south to the western end of Tabin Wildlife Reserve, where animals roam freely safe from the constant menace of poachers. He was very pleased to come across two banteng [6] grazing contentedly in the lush grass. These animals are of great concern to naturalists being the first large mammals in recent times to become almost extinct. He took several close-up photos of the bantengs-magnificent black animals with snow white legs. He did not delay as he was keen to reach Lahad Datu before sunset. He stayed at the Hotel Unimas in Jalan Seroja, near the Chinese temple. In the old days, Lahad Datu was a pirate den, home to the infamous Lanun brigades, who were pirates and slave traders. The hotel manager advised Adam to avoid the waterfront after dark. Next morning, he would be heading off into the great unknown, on the long trip to Tawau on the Indonesian border. He felt slightly apprehensive, partly because of the Lahad Datu's reputation for piracy and partly because his mind flashed back to the tragic story of the trader Walter Flint who 'disappeared' on the banks of the Kalabaking River in 1890. Still, he felt that he would be safe if he stayed on the National Expressway up to the Semporna junction, where he would head west, deep into Murut traditional land.

Next morning Adam made good time and reached the Semporna junction in just over an hour. There, he left the expressway, cut across the Tawau Hill National Park and a clutter of remote ulu villages and found himself in the land of the Tengara Muruts between the two muddy rivers, the Kwamut and the Kalabakang. The sun was hot and the air steamed up from the mudbanks and the jungle, hanging like a phosphorous vapour over the land. The only signs of life were the mosquitoes, the crocodiles basking like great logs in the tepid water, the distant call of the wah wahs and the rustle of wild pigs in the undergrowth.

It was here that Walter Flint [7] had a small shop in 1890. It was a general provision store selling tinned foods-cheese, sardines, biscuits, tea, sugar, flour, cooking oil, cigarettes and such like. Flint needed a companion so he married a young Murut girl, Lingud, having paid her father Numpal $125 as the bride price. However, Flint had not accustomed himself to the lifestyle of the Muruts. Their age-old tradition was 'your house is my house'. He was not well pleased when Lingud's parents and siblings moved in, consumed his food, spat betel juice over the floor and took supplies home with them in carrying baskets. It was the old problem of coping with marauding in-laws. Flint dealt with the problem like a true colonial. He persuaded Numpal and his family to go up the Nasan River and make a new clearing in the virgin jungle above the river's mouth. They agreed to do so and his wife went with them to establish a new and better settlement while he went down to Sandakan for a holiday. However, the devious Numpul, who owed Flint a considerable sum of money decided to do a runner. He and his family, including Lingud did not go to the new location. Instead, they headed south to the Kalabakang River. In this way, they severed ties with Flint, and Nunpal could offer Lingud for sale to the highest bidder. On his return, Flint discovered the deception. He was furious and set out to track down the fleeing in-laws. Eventually, he found them and there was a heated exchange as he demanded the return of his wife and his money. However, according to the Muruts, the journey had been too much for the white man. He became ill and died. They buried him near the river. However, his brother Ralph in Sandakan suspected foul play and set out with a party of 13 Dayak policemen on an expedition of enquiry.

When they reached Linidis on the Kalabakang River, they found Walter Flint's grave. They opened the grave and discovered that he had been decapitated. The search party then set off in search of Numpal and his guilty relatives. They found a fine longhouse down the Kalabakang River and a great celebration in progress. Rice beer was flowing freely, the gongs were beating, and the men were dancing and singing. Numpul was there with his wife and daughter. The expedition decided to go down the river and surprise the exulting Muruts. They approached the longhouse from the rear and opened fire from both ends. A bloody massacre followed. Some 130 Muruts were killed in the space of 20 minutes. The longhouse was razed to the ground. Only a few Muruts survived to tell the tale, including Lingud.

Adam was standing in the very spot where the killing occurred. The air was still and there was an eerie green glow in the sky. Then, he heard crackling in the undergrowth nearby. He assumed it was a wild boar or some other forest animal. More rustling followed and he got the unmistakable smell of clove-scented cigarettes. Suddenly, he was surrounded by five men who appeared out of nowhere. They carried guns so Adam thought they must be hunters on a pig hunt. They greeted Adam in Malay but spoke to each other in an unknown tongue. It took Adam a few minutes to realize that he was the prey. His captors turned out to be really pleasant, almost apologetic. They were members of Abu Sayyaf [8] with headquarters in Jolo in the Sulu Islands. Hijacking western travellers and Filipino Christians for ransom was their game. The leader of the gang was Abu Sambat, a chain-smoking warrior with a face like a baked potato. He told Adam: 'Don't worry. We not bad guys. We normally not kill people. You see, a dead body has no value.' Adam was not at all reassured by the word 'normally'. The other members of the gang all looked alike-small of stature, their bodies bronzed by the sun, with bulging sloe eyes and long black hair glistening with coconut oil. Abu Sambat explained that they were freedom fighters, not terrorists. They were not jihadists, just Muslim separatists. They certainly did not look like the poker-faced terrorists in the Hollywood movie, *Jihadists in Paradise.*

Adam quickly discovered that Abu Sambat was keen to discover the market value of his captive but there was no way Adam was going to tell him that he was an engineer with Murphy Oil. Instead, he pretended to be a drifter, down on his luck, working as a pastry chef in a Labuan hotel. He had few possessions, only RM 600 in cash.

'Ok' said Abu Sambat 'I speak to my boss in Jolo.' Adam waited in some trepidation for the outcome, hoping that Abu Sambat was telling his boss that they were not going to get much out of this lone rider who had little in the way of cash. What to do? They all sat down and over coffee and cigarettes a deal was hammered out. Adam would be released unharmed and taken to Tawau, where he would catch a boat back to KK. Sadly, the organization was very short of funds and needed to raise money by selling Adam's bike, his Pentax camera and his Tag Heuer watch. They would not take his money since he needed it to pay for his passage home, nor would they take his wedding ring. There was honour even among thieves. Adam protested. He wanted to complete his grand tour of Sabah; he needed his bike and he needed his camera which contained a record of his trip and pictures for his daughter. 'Sorry, Tuan. I have to follow the orders from my boss. You can have the film but we must keep the camera and the bike. How much you pay for the bike?' he asked. Adam told him it cost RM 22,000 and he explained that the bike was not really his. He had obtained a bank loan to buy it and he was paying RM500 a month.

'But you have insurance, so you can make a claim and get a new bike for free,' said Abu Sambat and that was that.

'Am I free to go now?' asked Adam.

'It is so, Tuan,' replied Abu Sambat.

They shook hands and thus ended Adam's great adventure. He was driven to Tawau and dropped off near the ferry terminal. He caught the ferry to KK and a second ferry to Labuan. On reflection, he was glad that unlike the luckless Walter Flint he had not lost his head on the banks of the Kalabakang River. He concluded that solo travel was not a good idea in eastern Sabah and he fully agreed with the wise words of his good friend Haji Omar: 'The most important thing in life is to stay alive.'

ENDNOTES:

1 *Forest:* Nottingham Forest Football Club

2 *houri:* A beautiful young woman, especially one in the Muslim Paradise.

3 *The Chartered Company:* In 1878, Alfred Dent formed the British North Borneo Chartered Company. He visited the Sultan of Sulu in 1881 and negotiated the lease of the territory that forms most of present-day Sabah to the Chartered Company for an annual sum 5,000 Straits dollars. And so, for 6 years, (1882 – 1888) the state of Sabah was owned and run by a British company. Then it became a Crown protectorate in 1888, known as British North Borneo but it continued to be administered by the Chartered Company for 60 years.

4 *James Brooke:* See R. Reece (1993). *The Name of Brooke.*

5 *Ranau death marches:* In January 1945, 455 Allied POWs were forced to march all the way from Sandakan to Ranau to act as labourers. Only half of the POWs made it to Ranau where they died of illness, malnutrition and ill-treatment. See: Lynette Silver. *Sandakan: A Conspiracy of Silence.*

6 *banteng:* Wild cattle on the endangered list after years of poaching and encroachment on their natural habitat. They are now a protected species in Tabin Wildlife Reserve and Malua Forest Reserve in Sabah.

7 *Walter Flint:* The story of the Walter Flint and his brother Raffles appears in *Land Below the Wind,* chapter 12.

8 *Abu Sayyaf:* A kidnap-for-ransom gang, affiliated to the Moro Liberation Front in Mindanao and the Sulu Islands.

4
THE MAN WHO MARRIED A BIRD

Pak Johari, who lived in Subang Jaya in Selangor,[1] was in his 50s when he decided to marry his second wife as he was perfectly entitled to do. In his religion, Islam, a man may have four wives as long as he can provide for all of them and treat them with equanimity. However, Pak Johari was not rich enough to support more than one wife so he divorced his first wife with whom he was having a hard time. She was constantly pestering him for money or jewellery or cosmetics and such luxury goods that are beyond the reach of a humble policeman with a teenage daughter at college and a mortgage round his neck. Besides, his wife Nabila had grown almost as wide as she was long and Pak Johari much preferred the tall slender type of woman.

During the fasting month of Ramadan, Pak Johari had business in the city of Medan in Indonesia. Medan is a beautiful city and it is said that the most beautiful women in Indonesia come from there. It was there that Pak Johari first laid eyes on the beautiful Alvira who was working as a sales lady in a large supermarket. He knew her name was Alvira because all the sales staff wore name tags. When Pak Johari and Alvira came face to face there was an instant click of understanding-a mutual attraction that neither of them had any control over. Even though they did not touch, they both felt an instant genetic bonding that is beyond the power of words to describe or explain. It was a brief encounter but somehow Alvira's image embedded itself in Pak Johari's brain and all that evening she could see nothing else but her image before his eyes. It was much more than a momentary flirtation; it was a total obsession and as he left the supermarket, he glanced back and saw in Alvira's languid eyes and on her face a beatific smile which seemed to say: 'Come with me and be my love.' A woman speaks with her eyes and Pak Johari read the message clearly. It was a look of love, a cry of passion, an imploration made with tears. Pak Johari was smitten by the demon of love.

It is not uncommon for men in their prime to experience a fatal attraction, quite often under the radar with a mistress. But Pak Johari wanted more than a mistress; he wanted a wife. He wanted a kind and gentle soul to enrich his dreary life and not a vicious woman with the temperament of a Rottweiler. However, he reasoned that should he marry again, it would be prudent for him to marry a Malay woman from his home state Selangor. There was an undercurrent of hostility towards Indonesians in Malaysia and Pak Johari feared that his daughter Misha might resent his marrying a foreign woman. 'But wait. I mustn't get ahead of myself. The lady may have other plans and it seems likely that a woman of such surpassing beauty would have a lot of male admirers.'

Pak Johari spent that evening in a bar hoping that a good binge would extinguish his passion, but in fact, it had the opposite effect and as he left the bar around midnight, he was heard exclaiming to all and sundry 'I will not marry an Indonesian temptress.' Of course, nobody paid the slightest attention to the drunken Pak Johari. It was well known that Malaysian men frequented Madan for booze and women, both of which were freely available.

Next day, Pak Johari returned to the supermarket not to buy anything in particular but to see the lovely Alvira once more. And sure enough, there she was at her checkout, looking as beguiling as ever. Long before he reached her, Pak Johari could feel her gaze upon him. It transfixed him to the marrow of his bones. He bought a few toiletries, not that he needed them, but to give his visit some credibility. As he joined the queue of shoppers at Alvira's checkout, he wanted to rush up to her, grab her in his arms and say: 'I love you. Marry me.' But of course, in a Muslim country, one does not do such crazy things. Instead, he wrote his name and mobile number on a piece of paper and pressed it into Alvira's hand as he was checking out.

Pak Johari had hardly reached the hotel when his mobile rang. It was the divine voice of the goddess Alvira. She told him that she wanted to see him later that day after work. She explained that it was not proper for her to visit him in his hotel but she would meet him in a downtown restaurant. She confessed that she found Pak Johari 'extremely interesting' and if it was the will of Allah, perhaps their chance encounter might develop into a 'meaningful relationship.'

Pak Johari could hardly believe his good fortune. Alvira seemed just as eager to meet him as he was to meet her. He set to work at once on preparing himself for his rendezvous with Alvira. He went to a barber, had a haircut and shampoo and had his graying hair tinted black. He then bought himself a dark shiny Chinese-made suit and a matching maroon necktie. That evening, as Pak Johari left the hotel, he looked like a dashing Romeo, his tall body honed to perfection by daily drill and exercise. He then made his way to Casa Kopitiam, a noted seafood restaurant where he had a beer while he waited for Alvira. It was not long before she arrived, looking as alluring as ever in a figure-hugging kebaya with matching red handbag and red leather shoes. She embraced Pak Johari and remarked: 'You are looking even more handsome than I had imagined. I hope you are enjoying your stay in our city. It is nice and cool here at this time of year.' Pak Johari was indeed enjoying his stay and that evening he and Alvira dined off chilli crab and lobster – a truly delightful meal. The restaurant was full of well-dressed young couples, all sipping glasses of Chianti or Jacob's Creek. In such a romantic setting, one thing can quickly lead to another and two perfect strangers can suddenly become lovers. We do not know exactly what transpired in that long after-dinner conversation but it appears that Pak Johari made it clear to Alvira that he wished to take their relationship 'to the next level'. Obviously, there were a few formal matters that needed attending to, but Pak Johari had good friends in Immigration and he was confident that once he and Alvira were married, she would be given PR status in Malaysia.

The next day, Pak Johari returned to his home in Subang, a link house overlooking the lake. He did all the things that a man does prior to marriage – renovating his house, buying new furniture, drapes and bed linen and exchanging his old battered Proton for a spanking new Honda Civic. For the first time in many a long year, Pak Johari was seen dashing about in a frenzy of activity, making sure everything in his house was fit for the goddess Alvira.

The wedding ceremony took place in Medan with all the colour and splendor of an Indonesian wedding. Even though he was in his 50s, everyone regarded Pak Johari as a suitable partner for the much younger Alvira, whose father was much relieved that his daughter, now 28, had at last found her man. He knew instinctively that Pak Johari was a good man, a gentleman and a true Muslim brother who would love and respect Alvira and give her a good life in Malaysia.

On their return to Malaysia, Pak Johari and Alvira spent many happy days and weeks getting to know each other and sharing a love that was as deep as the sea and as delicate as the silks and batiks that Alvira wore. For Pak Johari, all of this married bliss was heaven on earth and when he and Alvira made love, the earth moved. It was the perfect marriage-a marriage of true minds and the consummation of true love.

However, Alvira kept a dark secret from her husband. She did not tell him that she was really a bird. As soon as Pak Johari went to work, she would go to her room and sing:

> I am, I am, I am,
> The black swan of Medan
> Look upon my plume sublime,
> And marvel at my shape divine.

> I am, I am, I am
> The black swan of Medan,
> Alvira is my human name,
> And black magic is my game.

After singing her song, two wings would emerge and two webbed feet. Then she sang the same song again:

> I am, I am, I am,
> The black swan of Medan
> Look upon my plume sublime,
> And marvel at my shape divine.

As she was singing, feathers would appear and she would take the form of a beautiful swan. Once more she sang her song and this time a long neck and bill appeared. Then she would fly out of the window and go to the Subang lake in search of fish and crabs. When Pak Johari returned from work, he would find his loving wife in the kitchen preparing his evening meal and neither he nor anyone else knew that his wife was really a swan.

However, his daughter Misha, who lived nearby with her mother, felt that there was something odd about Alvira. She had heard many stories about Indonesian women using black magic to do extraordinary things. She suspected that her stepmother was up to something so she arranged to spy on her from the house next door. And to her great astonishment, she heard Alvira sing her song and turn into a swan which then flew out of the window towards the lake. In order to make sure that that she was not dreaming, Misha rang Alvira's doorbell but there was no response. The bird had flown.

'Merciful Allah, the lady is really a swan-a hantu [2] in human form,' she exclaimed. She lost no time in dashing to her father's office to tell him of the vision she had just witnessed. At first, Pak Johari refused to believe a word she told him. Possibly she was lying, or consuming an illegal substance. The streets of Kuala Lumpur were awash with syabu.[3] However, when Misha swore that her every word was true, he too decided to spy on Alvira.

Next day, he went to work as usual but returned shortly afterwards and hid in the house next door. It was not long until he heard the sweet strains of Alvira's song:

> I am, I am, I am,
> The black swan of Medan
> Look upon my plume sublime,
> And marvel at my shape divine.

Then the black swan flew out of the window and made straight for Subang lake. 'Merciful Allah, it's true. I've married a bird!' exclaimed Pak Johari in anguish. He shook his head in disbelief like a man who had just seen a ghost. It took his quite some time to recover his composure. One reads about such paranormal things in the New Straits Times and one sees documentaries about ghosts and haunted houses on television, but this was no fantasy. His beautiful wife was a black swan. This was more than an embarrassing predicament; it was a complete catastrophe. In such a situation decisive action is paramount. He would have to terminate the bitch, otherwise all over Selangor he would be known henceforth as the man that married a bird.

When he returned home that evening, his loving wife embraced him as usual, then went to the kitchen to fetch his evening meal. Meanwhile, Pak Johari went to the tool shed and got his parang.[4] Then, he went into the kitchen, bolted the door and windows and began singing Alvira's song:

> I am, I am, I am,
> The black swan of Medan, etc.

Alvira was struck dumb. She tried in vain to stop her husband from singing but she dare not approach him as he had a fierce look in his eyes and he was brandishing his parang menacingly. As soon as Pak Johari began singing, Alvira slowly transformed into a swan. She tried to escape but all exits were sealed. She then made for Pak Johari, screeching like a demented unicorn. However, with one mighty blow of his parang, Pak Johari severed her head and her writhing body soon expired on the cold stone floor. And that was the end of the beautiful Alvira.

ENDNOTES:

1 *Selangor*: One of the 13 states that make up the Federation of Malaysia. The Sultan of Selangor is one of nine sultans who were powerful rulers during the colonial era 1875-1957. The Sultans still retain certain royal prerogatives as set out in Article 38 of the Malaysian Constitution. Selangor is situated on the west coast of Peninsular Malaysia, encircling the capital Kuala Lumpur

2 *hantu:* ghosts, spirits, the undead. See Danny Lim (2008). *The Malaysian Book of the Undead*. Kuala Lumpur: Matahari Books.

3 *syabu:* the drug amphetamine

4 *parang:* a machete

5
KONDOR, THE ROYAL TIGER

During the 19th century, waves of Chinese workers migrated to the Malay States, which were then part of the British Empire. The Teochew came from Guangdong (formerly Canton), the Hokkien from Fukien, the Hakka from Nan Ling and the Hainanese from the island of Hainan. Initially, they came as indentured labourers to work in the tin mines of Perak and the rubber plantations of Malacca. However, they also engaged in trade and set up trading posts all over the Straits Settlements[1] and the Federated Malay States. They traded in various commodities, especially opium, spices and traditional medicines. They were hawkers, pawnbrokers, goldsmiths and shop owners. They soon dominated the commercial life in many states, selling sundry goods and services. Every town had a Chinatown full of general stores and coffeehouses, famous for 'kai fan',[2] Chow Mein, Won Ton Soup and other Chinese dishes.

In the late late 1870s, the town of Papan was one of the main tin mining towns in Perak. Thousands of Chinese miners, traders and businessmen made Papan their home. It soon became 'the tin capital of the world', having replaced Larut as the main tin producer in Perak. By the turn of the century, Papan had become a prosperous town, which had two distinct populations-the Chinese and the Mandailing community from Sumatra. Its wide streets had rows of shophouses above which the owners lived in roomy apartments behind latticed windows. There were temples, clubs, coffeehouses, medicine halls and even brothels in the town.

One of the earliest traders to move to Papan was Ong Poh Sing. He was a trader in traditional Chinese medicines. Whatever the illness, Ong

Poh had a cure for it, be it gastric pain, bowel disorder, lumbago, stiff neck, arthritis, erectile dysfunction, etc. One of Ong Poh's most sought after products was 'yellow man'.[3] Only Ong Poh and his sons knew the formula of the famous 'yellow man'; it was a closely guarded secret but it was said to be a concoction make in part from the chemical in the yellow spice turmeric and the stewed brain of monkey. It was believed to be a powerful restorative medicine, the elixir of life and man's best friend long before the goji berry[4] and Tongkat Ali[5] had become popular. Yellow man, like opium, was traded as a commodity from Shanghai to Singapore and Ong Poh became one of the richest men in Perak.

Ong Poh was a man of few words but great learning. He was well versed in the Analects of Confucius and his science was based on observation of natural phenomena. He dedicated his life to the study of herbal life and the promotion of good mental and bodily health. He was steeped in Chinese lore, astrology, feng shui,[6] and calligraphy. He was proud of his Chinese origin, culture and language but he also advocated and fostered hospitality and good relations with the Mandailing people who were Muslims from Sumatra.

Because of poor sanitation and diet, the people of Papan succumbed to diseases such as malaria, dysentery, cholera and consumption. Working conditions in the mines were simply appalling and the miners suffered greatly from respiratory diseases by daily exposure to toxic fumes in the mines. In addition, accidents were common and miners were sometimes buried alive when a shaft collapsed. Mr. Ong had a ready market for his medicines and tonics. However, he was not a mean man and if a person was poor, no payment was expected.

At that time, the penghulu[7] of Papan was Rajah Bilah. He lived in some style in the Rumah Bilah, a palatial mansion made of concrete and local hardwood. Rajah Bilah and his nobles were the ruling class and enjoyed a cordial relationship with the British administration. Ong Poh was a frequent visitor to the palace where his services were much in demand by Rajah Bilah's extended family. It was here that Rajah Bilah and his many wives and children, led a life of indolence and ease far removed from the harsh realities of life outside.

To mark Rajah Bilah's 50th birthday, his devoted wife Tenghu Sonita decided to present him with a Sumatran tiger, which in Malay culture is a symbol of power and good fortune. The presentation of the tiger would mark the end of a week of celebration. Of course, the event had to be kept secret from Rajah Bilah until the appointed day. Great care was lavished on the splendid tiger that had been shipped all the way from Sumatra. It was kept in isolation some distance from the palace and it was pampered so as to be in peak condition for the presentation ceremony which would be open to the whole Papan community.

Unfortunately, the tiger became ill. It lay listless in its den for hours on end in obvious pain. Ong Poh was summoned to diagnose the problem and hopefully restore the tiger to good health. The poor tiger seemed to be suffering from a wasting disease; its eyes were bloodshot and it walked with a limp. It was off its food and spent hours motionless and seemingly in great pain. Ong Poh soon discovered a tumour in its groin. There was no veterinary surgeon in the area and he was not quite sure whether he should undertake to cure the tiger because should he fail, or worse still, should tiger die, his reputation would be in tatters. At the same time, he could not just walk away, out of respect for Rajah Bilah and Tengku Sonita. It was a complex problem for all concerned. Tengku Sonita made it clear that the tiger must be cured at any cost since were it to die, its demise would be construed as an omen of ill fortune, with disastrous consequences for the ruling family. Rajah Bilah was the 'tiger' of his people and his well-being and prosperity would be undermined should the tiger die.

Ong Poh knew that time was of the essence. He had only a few weeks to restore the tiger to good health and he felt sorry for the poor animal, which looked weak and forlorn and seemed to have given up the ghost. However, he was confident that daily doses of his magical 'yellow man' would restore the animal to good health. First of all, he would have to sedate the tiger and then inject it with a strong antibiotic. He would massage the affected area with juniper liniment and finally he would mix 'yellow man' with meat extract for the tiger to eat. It was some time before the tiger actually began to eat and to Ong Poh's delight, it devoured the food and looked well pleased. At that stage, he had no means of knowing whether the tumour was malignant or not. He assumed that it was nonmalignant and most probably caused by tick bites.

Ong Poh attended to the tiger several times each day and he was pleased to notice a gradual improvement in its condition. Its appetite and mobility improved each passing day and the tumour seemed less prominent. The medicine was definitely working and he could discern a spring in the tiger's step and a brightness in its amber eyes. It even became frisky and playful but Ong Poh was careful to maintain a safe distance since the tiger was raised in the wild and unused to captivity. He always addressed the tiger in Malay as if that was its mother tongue and he called it Kondor. After a while, the tiger seemed to recognize its name and its royal status. Ong Poh was fascinated by its demeanour and its awesome beauty. He was well pleased with Kondor's steady progress but he was careful not to make any rash predictions about its imminent recovery.

In fact, he knew quite well that Kondor was winning the battle for survival. Each day, he noticed some improvement in its condition and appearance. However, the wily Ong Poh made out that the tiger was still in mortal danger and that its chances of survival were minimal. Poor Tengku Sonita was beside herself with grief. It seemed that nothing short of a miracle was needed to cure the tiger. It was no ordinary tiger but one that was destined to become a member of the royal household. Everyone except Rajah Bilah spent sleepless nights, waiting anxiously for good news, but Ong Poh was running out of time. Rajah Bilah's birthday was but a week away and preparations were under way for the great event.

'Please, please, I beg you, save the tiger!' Tengku Sonita pleaded with Ong Poh, her voice choked with sadness. He promised to do all that was humanly possible but he conceded that the tiger's fate was in the hands of the gods of the forest. One evening, he informed Tengku Sonita that he would like to conduct a healing rite, based on an old Chinese tradition, to seek divine intervention. He would inject the tiger with morpheme to sedate it, then recite an age-old mantra and sprinkle the animal with holy water and if it was the will of the gods of the forest, the tiger would either be cured or left to die. After much discussion with her nobles, Tengku Sonita agreed that Ong Poh's proposal was the only option.

Next day, Tengku Sonita and most of the royal household attended the healing ritual which in Ong Poh's words was the last throw of the dice. She watched closely as he approached Kondor. He was accompanied by several red-robed young Chinese men bearing lighted joss sticks and chanting an ancient Chinese mantra to the muffled tones of a drum. It was sheer drama as Ong Poh and his men approached a rather hostile Kondor, who obviously viewed the whole proceedings with apprehension. He snarled and pawed the ground to warn the intruders to keep their distance. The royal retinue waited and watched with bated breath. Gradually, Ong Poh made contact with Kondor and after much coaxing, he fed the tiger his daily dose of meat extract laced with 'yellow man'. Then he injected Kondor with morpheme and very soon the animal slumped forward and lay prone on its back. The royal members watched with growing concern. Then Ong Poh and his men circled the prostrate tiger, chanting their mantra in the most hideous voice imaginable. The scent of burning incense filled the air and ominous black clouds darkened the sky. Then, he bent over the tiger and injected it with a reviver. He requested the gathering to count down. It was the moment of truth. The tiger would either jump up cured or roll over and die. Everyone stood and counted down, 10, 9, 8... Ong Poh orchestrated the count and as everyone roared 'zero', Kondor suddenly stirred and leaped up showing all the ferocity of a ferocious tiger. The assembled onlookers cheered and Tengku Sonita wept with joy. Ong Poh and his red-robed assistants bowed and left the enclosure grateful that the gods of the forest had been appeased. Kondor, now restored to good health, was duly presented to Rajah Bilah on his 50th birthday. He confessed that he had never seen such a fine-looking animal.

Ong Poh's standing in the palace was greatly enhanced and he enjoyed royal patronage for the rest of his days. Only he knew that the tiger's miraculous cure was something that had been mainly staged and arranged. However, he did not see it as a deception since at least initially there was always the chance that the tiger might not respond to this magic treatment. His old apothecary in Main Street, Papan, still stands and on the wall is a faded sepia photograph of Ong Poh feeding Kondor a dish of meat and 'yellow man'.

Sadly, today Papan is a ghost town. Its streets are derelict, the mines are exhausted and all that remains is the lore of the great mining days of Papan and the Kinta Valley.

ENDNOTES:

1   *Straits Settlements*: The former British Crown Colony established in 1867. It comprised Singapore, Penang, Malacca and later included Labuan.
2   *kai fan*: chicken soup
3   *yellow man*: The popular name for Ong's traditional Chinese medicine.
4   *goji berry*: A red berry of the boxthorn family widely used in China and Tibet to boost the immune system
5   *Tongkat Ali:* Traditional medicine made from the roots of the Tongkat Ali plant. It is the most used herb in Southeast Asia, famous for its male-enhancing properties.
6   *feng shui:* In Chinese thought, a system of laws governing spatial arrangement and orientation in relation to the flow of energy (chi).
7   *Rajah Bilah* was penghulu of the Mandailings in Perak, 1875-1911. He was a British-appointed headman, revenue-collector and peace-keeper.

ENSLAVED BY LOVE

Lisa Lowe came from Taiping,[1] the wettest town in Malaysia, but that was long ago. When I first met her, she was a vocalist at various clubs in Kuala Lumpur (KL). Sometimes she'd do a stint in Kota Kinabalu, or Kuching or Singapore but her regular work was at clubs in KL, especially those in Jalan P. Ramlee and Bangsar. Thanks to the generosity of the Arts Council, she obtained a bursary to study music and dance at the Swan School of Music and Dance in London. Lisa was born to sing. Music lovers were enraptured by her languid voice and her enthralling presence on stage. Her ambition was to be a music-hall vocalist and to earn a living by singing at clubs and functions in Kuala Lumpur.

Although of slight build, Lisa had a powerful voice but she still had to learn how to project her voice across the vast expanse of an auditorium and she also had to learn how to perform in the studio in front of the television camera. At that time, in the early 80s, live music shows were popular on Malaysian television and the old days of the music hall had given way to a new generation of solo artists and groups who performed like prima donnas at exclusive clubs. Lisa had all the making of a great star. Her soulful voice was said to resemble that of Edith Piaf.[2] She had that rare quality of producing a quiver that sent a chill down the spine – the emotional contact beyond the words and the music, between the voice of the performer and the ears of the listener. It was said that she 'sang like an angel' and since nobody has ever heard an angel sing, we can presume that the phrase means that she sang with an ethereal and mystic quality that one associates with a songstress like Enya,[3] singing one of her haunting songs in Gaelic.

Lisa wanted to be a performer of modern dance as well as a singer. Her dance teacher was a certain Miss Cynthia Morris who developed a programme of semi-classical dance movements based on old Celtic themes. The dance routines were done barefoot with minimal clothing to the beat of an ensemble of fiddles, tin whistles and bodhrans.[4] Lisa saw dance as a means of liberating women and as a way of developing the aesthetic sensibilities of ordinary women. She sought to capture on stage the grace and beauty of her native land – the sounds of the rainforest, the colours of the kampung,[5] the wind that rustles in the pomelo trees and the dark magic of the hantu[6] that roam abroad after dark. For her, music and dance were a means of expression – a liberating force, as potent and variable as speech. Under Miss Moss' tutorship, she learned to improvise to music, to compose steps, to work in groups and to choreograph dance sequences based on the myths and lore of Malay, Chinese and Indian culture. Dance and music merged women of different ethnic origin into one seamless Malaysian persona.

Lisa did several shows in London with the BBC Dance Orchestra and her songs, while not reaching a mass audience, were popular on radio and two to them were recorded on the Crown label. It was in London that Lisa met Adam Zachariah, a medical student at the College of Surgeons. Adam was a Eurasian [7] from Malacca. He spoke fluent English, Malay, and Chinese as well as the local Portuguese dialect, Cristang. They were an unlikely pair, coming from different worlds and cultures yet from the start they were drawn magnetically to each other. Adam was tall, dark and handsome, with jet black hair and a neatly trimmed moustache that gave him a distinguished bearing. He was affable and witty with a keen sense of humour. There was something haunting about his voice which was deep and smooth with traces of an English accent. It was rare for Lisa to meet a man who seemed to have it all – good looks, a promising medical career, a pleasant and unassuming manner and clearly a man of some means. Adam likewise found Lisa irresistible. She had a certain mystic quality that professional men seek in a spouse. She had a sparkle in her lustrous hazel eyes and her long auburn hair gave her the appearance of a Celtic goddess. In a crowd, Lisa always stood out because of her unmistakable showbiz sheen.

Each weekend, Lisa and Adam would dine in one of the many Malaysian restaurants that one finds in London. Like most Malaysians, they were great talkers and they spent many happy hours together in conversation. Their deep love of each other evolved out of their sustained verbal interaction. They bewitched each other with their stories and it soon became obvious that one day they would march down the aisle of St. Francis Xavier church in Malacca.

On their return to Malaysia in 1986, they got married and went to live in Kuala Lumpur. Adam was employed as a junior doctor at the University Hospital in Petaling Jaya and Lisa was in demand at various show venues in the capital as well as on television. Life was going according to plan and they each prospered in their chosen careers. They lived in some style in an exclusive villa complex in Mount Kiara and apart from the daily torture of driving to work in congested Kuala Lumpur, their life was one of bliss. At that time, doctors who qualified overseas had to spend five years in government service before being allowed to go into private practice. Adam was eventually offered a partnership with an Indian colleague at a private clinic in Petaling Jaya. His partner was Dr. Sunil Kumar, a Malaysian of Indian origin from Klang. He was a devout Catholic and every Sunday he would take Adam and Lisa to St. Anne's Church in Port Klang. It was reported that miracles were a regular occurrence at the church and several miraculous cures were attributed to the intercession of St. Anne. Even those with incurable diseases continued to frequent the Sunday service and found the inner peace and resilience to suffer misfortune without yielding to despair.

Then, in 1996, disaster struck. Adam was diagnosed with Parkinson's disease. Early that year, he began to exhibit the usual symptoms of the disease – a slight tremor of the right hand which later spread to both sides of the body causing stiffness and weakness as well as trembling of the muscles. He was no longer able to attend to his patients. His mind was unaffected but his speech became slow and hesitant. He could still read and write but his handwriting became very small. He was no longer fit enough to continue in partnership with Dr. Kumar, who understood his plight and stood by him providing all the assistance that medical science could offer. Both he and the neurosurgeons at the hospital knew they could not cure Adam's condition but they could arrest its development by therapeutic drugs. Fortunately for Adam, he had a life insurance policy which meant that he and Lisa would be well provided for financially. The problem was how a highly active man like Adam could cope with the stress of being reduced to inaction. There were days when he felt like a caged lion. He was no longer able to play a game of golf nor to umpire cricket matches, which he loved to do. It was sheer torture for him to adjust to a sedentary life. Still, he managed to come to terms with his affliction. He no longer brooded over it but accepted it as the will of God. He was determined not to let Parkinsonism rule his life.

Adam was fortunate that he had a loving wife totally dedicated to his well-being. Moreover, he had access to the best medical care at the hospital and regular visits from his colleague Dr. Kumar who was well versed in the treatment of Parkinson's disease which was a subject he had explored in his graduation paper at the College of Surgeons several years previously. What surprised Adam was the sudden onset of the disease and the fact that he was in his prime, just 45 years old. He knew that that he was ill but he was not disabled. He was able to wash and dress himself and make himself a cup of tea, take his dog for a walk, drive to the Royal Selangor Club and play a game of chess. He would spend a lot of time reading his favourite books or listening to his collection of classical music. He never complained about his condition and he seemed immune to pain. He spent many hours each week communicating by email with his many relatives and friends. His life revolved around his laptop. His dog Kaya and his two cats were his constant companions.

All those years, Lisa stood by her man. She put aside her own musical career and performed only on special occasions such as Christmas, Hari Raya and Chinese New Year. She knew that there was no cure for Parkinson's disease and that sufferers were prone to become depressed. There was no way she was going to allow the man she loved to succumb to depression. She supervised his daily dosage of medications, which as the disease progressed became quite complex because several different types of drugs needed to be administered in various combinations. As devastating and unpredictable as the disease was, it invoked in Lisa a fighting spirit to move mountains to help her man. Her dedication and unconditional love made his daily battle bearable.

Lisa spent hours each day preparing Adam's favourite food. He had a passion for seafood and homemade vegetarian soups. He enjoyed very much having Dr. Kumar and his family to dinner. Adam remained as witty as ever and he became very animated when the political situation was discussed. He had an abiding hatred of corruption, cronyism and nepotism, the hallmarks of Malaysian politics at that time. He referred in jest to the ruling coalition as the 'The Brotherhood of Bandits'. Of course, mocking the government is a natural pastime in Malaysia and nobody ever expected politicians to work on behalf of the rakyat [8] but in their own self-interest. While people in the UK entertain themselves by watching banal shows like 'Coronation Street' and 'East Enders' on television, Malaysians prefer to amuse themselves by discussing the latest political scandals and dirty tricks. One particular feature of Malaysian politics is 'frog-hopping', that is, hopping from one political party to another. It is a fascinating aspect of Malaysian life where political scandals are the normal topic of conversation. And, on that subject, Malaysia was top of the league in Southeast Asia.

As the years went by, Adam's condition deteriorated. His mobility became uncertain and he walked with unbalanced shuffling steps. He moved with a permanent rigid stoop. Eating, washing, dressing and other everyday activities became progressively more challenging. For instance, he could no longer bend down to tie his shoe laces and his right hand trembled so much that that dare not shave. But Lisa shaved and washed him every day. Moreover, she massaged his stiff limbs using Indian oils and lotions that she obtained from Dr. Kumar. All this time, Adam remained alert and cheerful. Lisa was astonished at his ready wit and his unfailing good humour. He always had a kind word for his devoted wife who did not act out of duty or compassion but out of love. She never once felt the need to go away and take a break from minding her ailing husband. She had no desire to be part of the rich social life of Kuala Lumpur which she had previously enjoyed. Instead, her whole life revolved around Adam and his disablement. She tried to remain cheery and upbeat on the outside while crying within. For her, those years of caring for the man she loved were a blessing from the Lord. She felt no resentment whatever in being saddled with the daily cross of caring for another. Her loving response to Adam's pain and suffering sublimated her whole life and elevated her to a higher state of consciousness. It was a paradox of sorts; the starry-eyed Lisa found peace and fulfillment in the midst of misfortune. Every evening after supper, Lisa would read from the Bible to Adam. She loved the Psalms – the songs of David-and they both prayed the rosary together and a special prayer to St. Anne. The once agnostic Lisa gradually rediscovered the faith that she had been raised in at the Holy Faith convent school.

Sadly, Adam died in 2002 at his home. He died peacefully in his sleep. The previous night he had complained of severe chest pains and fearing a heart attack, Lisa has summoned Dr. Kumar. There was little he could do, however and he and Lisa could see before their eyes Adam's life ebbing away. Father Anslem was called to administer the last rites. Adam died as he had lived, with a smile on his face. If ever a man was fit to appear before his Maker, it was Adam Zachariah. His funeral Mass was attended by hundreds of Malaysians of different religions and none. They all agreed with the word spoken by Father Anslem about the heroic life of Adam: 'He does not die whose good name lives on.'

Adam was buried in the family vault in Malacca. As for Lisa, she was inconsolable yet resigned to the will of God. She felt that part of her had died that day with her loving husband, but she would never forget his last words before he closed his eyes in the sleep of death: 'The Lord giveth, and the Lord taketh away; blessed be the name of the Lord.' (Job 1:21) Those words were an amazing testimony to his faith; a just man steadfast to the end in spite of adversity. Lisa could not bear to live alone in Kuala Lumpur and she moved to Malacca so as to be near the resting place of the man who had transformed her life. She still talked to him daily and visited his grave regularly where she was often seen singing a sad song of love and remembrance.

ENDNOTES:

1   *Taiping*: A town in northern Perak, the wettest town in Malaysia.
2   *Edith Piaf:* The famous cabaret and music-hall singer in the late 1930s. One of her famous songs was 'Je ne regrette rien.'
3   *Enya:* A famous Irish soul singer
4   *bodhrán*: A shallow one-sided Irish drum, played with a short stick with knobbed ends. Plural: a 'botheration' of bodhrans'!
5   *kampung*: the Malay word for village
6   *hantu:* ghosts / spirits /the undead
7   *Eurasian*: Of mixed European and Asian parentage. In Malaysia, Eurasians live mainly in Penang, Malacca and the Klang Valley.
8   *rakyat*: The common people, as opposed to their rulers.

7

THE BOMOH OF SUNGAI LIANG

One thing that the diverse races of Malaysia agree on is the existence of spirits or ghosts which are collectively known as hantu.[1] Spirits in Malaysia were normally named according to the form they took or the place they frequented and there are literally dozens of different types of hantu, such as Hantu Belangas, (crab spirit), Hantu Laut (sea spirit), Hantu Air (water spirit) etc. Some of the hantu are dangerous and unforgiving while others are benevolent or harmless. One of the most feared of the evil hantu is the dreaded Orang Minyak,[2] a serial rapist who went about stark naked smeared in oil in search of virgins.

Some years ago, while visiting Perlis, I stopped off for lunch at a small roadside café in Kampung Pangas. It was there that that I met the famous bomoh [3] Mat Ratu. Of course, I did not know that he was a bomoh and I was far from clear about the function and role of the bomoh in Malay society. He spoke little English and I spoke less Malay but somehow, we managed to communicate with some occasional translation by the café owner, a kind gentleman of Indian origin. Mat Ratu told me that he was a professional bomoh, the seventh son of a seventh son. He explained the nature of his work. One of his prime functions was to conduct seasonal rites in order to enlist the good fortune of the spirit world for a bountiful harvest, a very important matter since Perlis and Kedah are the rice bowl of Malaysia. A supplication ritual often involved sacrificing a chicken, a goat, or some other animal. It made good sense to maintain good relations with the hantu in one's locality and certainly the rural people of Perlis believed that the Semangat Padi [4] had the power to make the rice yield more abundant. Another function of the bomoh was that of medicine-man who prescribed herbal treatments for a wide range of illnesses from fever, to snake bite, to malaria, to dysentery etc. Whatever the medical problem, the bomoh had a cure for it. I decided to put Mat Ratu to the test on this matter. For several years, I had a small wart on my index finger, so I said to Mat Ratu: 'Can you get rid of my wart?' He replied instantly, 'Yes, can can'. He took a blade of lemon grass and wrapped it around my finger. Then he chanted a magic verse and he assured me that the wart would disappear as soon as the blade of lemon grass withered. He told me to place it under a stone and as soon as it decomposed, my wart would vanish. To my utter amazement, it worked. On my return to Subang, I duly placed the blade of lemon grass under a stone and several weeks later it had decomposed and was being devoured by red ants. The wart on my finger had disappeared without a trace.

Yet another function of the bomoh was that of ghostbuster. He had the power to track down and banish malicious spirits that perpetrated criminal acts such as plunder, cannibalism, abduction of persons and gross acts of indecency. Very often the spirits were really vampires or monsters and had to be banished by invoking black magic. Thus, according to Mat Ratu, the bomoh played a key role in Malay society mediating relations between the human and spiritual worlds. A bomoh's knowledge (ilmu) did not come out of books. It was innate and spiritually inherited. Much of Mat Ratu's 'ilmu' derived from the age-old beliefs and practice of the Mah-Meri tribe of the Orang Asli[5] in Selangor. Like the other indigenous people of the Malay peninsula and Borneo, they believed that spirits lurked in rivers, trees, caves and hills and if not appeased, they could bring illness, destruction and bad fortune. The Orang Asli believed that the ideal world was one in which the physical and spiritual elements were balanced. Mat Ratu belonged to a long line of bomohs and his skills as a ghostbuster were much in demand across Malaysia and Singapore.

Casting off evil spirits is an elaborate and risky undertaking. The initial problem is divining the exact location of the intruder. Very often it is a djinn on a vengeful mission who may be hiding under the floorboards or in a cupboard. For instance, a local lady had asked Mat Ratu to purge her house of an evil spirit. She felt it choking her every night whenever she went to sleep. Using a metal divining rod, he soon found the intruder hiding in a cupboard. Mat Ratu recited his ghostbusting incantation: 'Come forth spirit of darkness and begone from this place before the rising of the sun'. A creature resembling a shrouded corpse emerged. It was known locally as the Pocong ghost. It was said to be the soul of a dead person dressed in a white shroud. Then Mat Ratu recited another magic verse and sprinkled the ghost with holy water, whereupon it made off and disappeared into the bowels of the earth. That was a simple case of a delinquent spirit causing grief to a helpless woman. In such a simple case, Mat Ratu received a fee of RM 100. More difficult cases commanded prices reaching into the thousands.

Experienced bomohs like Mat Ratu had enhanced vision and sensitivity to spirits enabling them to detect malevolent energy emanating from certain quarters where a spirit was hiding. Just like sniffer dogs, they could pick up the peculiar musty scent of an intruder. I asked Mat Ratu to say exactly how these spirits smelt to him and he looked puzzled for a moment since smell is a difficult thing to describe. He said it was a pungent smell, something like the smell of a burning rag.

Mat Ratu told me about a recent exorcism that he conducted on a man he cured of a curse placed on him by a vengeful former lover. He was literally wasting away. He vomited blood, mosquitoes and metal filings for more than a year. Mat Ratu explained that he took this man outside his muddy hut, where he lit a ring of fire around him and having recited the required incantation, he instructed the man to step over it. The man was then soaked in a tub of herb-spiced water. The explanation for this curious ritual is simple. Fire burns away all evil from the body and water cleanses the soul.

Mat Ratu told me several horrific stories of his battles with the spirits of darkness that inhabited the rainforest, lakes, rivers and padi fields of Perlis. His most extraordinary case was his confrontation with the dreaded Orang Minyak of Sungai Liang, a local spirit known as Si Bongkok. One could hardly credit that such a demonic monster could be found in a quiet kampung on the banks of the Sungai Liang. Mat Ratu told me that the dreaded Si Bongkok had terrorised the residents of Kampung Pangas and surrounding villages for many months. According to local lore, Si Bangkok was once a hunchback. However, he did a Faustian deal with the devil to have him transformed into a handsome young man in return for raping 21 young virgins over a period of seven days.

At that point, I suggested that hantu, ghosts and monsters were the invention of simple rural folk to provide an explanation for natural phenomena. They were fictional creatures, I told him, just like Conan Doyle's *The Hound of the Baskervilles.*

'I wish it were so,' replied Mat Ratu 'but the hantu are real all right. Sure, amn't I tormented by them?' To prove his point, he told me how he had recently neutralised a Hungry Ghost who went about at night looking for food. This ghost would throw stones, gravel and used batteries at a house causing sleepless nights for its residents. He explained that this type of ghost is hungry for blood and in order to appease it, blood is drawn from a hen, mixed with water and then thrown up to the sky where the ghost will consume it. He had banished many a Hungry Ghost in that manner. The important thing was to know your enemy.

However, dealing with a monster like Si Bongkok was an entirely different matter. Mat Ratu would never forget his encounter with the monster. He knew only too well that Si Bongkok would be a formidable opponent, as evil as the devil incarnate and as slippery as a barrel of eels. He had previously dealt with a few similar cases on the East Coast and he knew that there was no end to the deviousness and malice of an ogre like Si Bongkok. Ogres are carnivores. They will eat any kind of flesh be it human, animal, fish or fowl. They eat seafood raw-crabs, lobsters, inshore fish and eels. Their food of choice is human flesh.

Si Bongkok was a thoroughly nasty fellow. He had the ability to transform into a handsome young man who would walk the streets at night looking for virgins to intimidate and seduce for sex. If they refused, as they usually did, he would cast a spell on them, rape them and not content with satisfying his lust, he would cut their throat and suck their blood. Finally, he would carve up the body into chunks which he carried off to his den.

It was a moonlit night as Mat Ratu approached the monster's den. He found him fast asleep on a limestone slab, snoring and belching in a most disgusting manner. As usual, Mat Ratu raised his eyes to heaven and invoked the assistance of the Lord of the Universe. Then, he took his blowpipe and a poisoned arrow. He took careful aim and the arrow pierced the ogre's right eye, causing him to leap up like a wounded lion.

He began stamping the ground in a paroxysm of rage. Once more, hidden behind a boulder above the ogre's den, Mat Ratu took aim and this time the poisoned arrow pierced the monster's left eye, leaving him totally blind. He foamed at the mouth and howled in a demented rage as the deadly poison was having its effect. Once more, Mat Ratu invoked the Lord of the Universe: 'Great Lord of the Universe, to whom all homage is due, let my poisoned arrow pierce the heart of the monster Si Bongkok and rid Sungai Liang of his foul deeds.' Then he made an offering of yellow rice, chicken bones and betel leaves and prostrated himself three times on the ground. Slowly and silently, he approached Si Bongkok who was lying face upwards, screaming in anguish and emitting a foul-smelling stench from his writhing belly. Mat Ratu steadied himself and shot a poisoned arrow straight into the monster's heart. Amid howls of anguish that rent the sill night air, Si Bongkok expired.

Mat Ratu returned to the village relieved that his mission had been successful. Word soon spread that Si Bongkok had been slain and the entire population rushed to the hillside to see for themselves that the ogre was now a corpse. They wept tears of joy and sent for Mat Ratu to thank him for the wondrous deed. Then they heaped dead branches and dried ox dung over Si Bongkok's body, soaked it in petrol and set it alight. The villages danced around the bonfire in a frenzy of delight. To this day, the visitor can see the blackened spot on the ground where Si Bongkok was cremated.

ENDNOTES:

1   *hantu:* spirits or ghosts. See Danny Lim (2008). *The Malaysian Book of the Undead.* Kuala Lumpur: Matahari Books

2   *Orang Minyak*: A repulsive ogre and serial rapist with a taste for blood. He would appear as a handsome young man who went about seeking virgins to rape and devour. A truly evil monster.

3   *bomoh*: The 'spirit doctor' or traditional medicine-man in the Malay States. He performs rituals to placate the hantu and he can cleanse a village of malignant spirits.

4   *Semangat padi*: rice spirits

5   *Orang Asli*: The indigenous people of peninsular Malaysia

ABU ONG, THE KING COBRA

The Orang Asli[1] are the forgotten people of Malaysia. They are the original people of the Malay Peninsula. They belong to two main tribes. The Semang or dark-skinned Negritos settled in the highlands of Kelentan, Terengganu and the Northern parts of Perak, Kedah and Pahang (Moon & Cubit, 2000). They have lived in the rainforest ever since and many of them still retain their nomadic lifestyle, living off the fruits of the forest. The other concentration of Orang Asli is the Senoi, or 'Sakai'. They settled in upland Perak, Pahang and Selangor. Related to the Senoi are the creative Mah Meri of coastal Selangor. They, just like the other Orang Asli, have retained their old cultural beliefs and practices. Many of them now live in settlements and some have converted to Christianity but still cling to their old animist beliefs. They live a totally organic life and have great respect for the rainforest and the many hantu[2] that inhabit it.

The rainforest is a rich source of food. It abounds in wildlife that is hunted by the Orang Asli such as wild boar, mouse deer, rodents, lizards and snakes. To the Orang Asli, snakes are a source of food. A five-metre-long cobra would feed a whole family for several days. It would be chopped up into chunks and cooked slowly for two hours making a delightful stew to which herbs and lemons grass were added as well as chilies, onions, peppers and beans. It was not only delicious but highly nutritious as well.

One of the most cherished values of the Orang Asli community is a strong belief in spirits. According to them, in the rainforest, you never walk alone. The forest is the home of the undead – the hantu, ghosts and djinn. Western people do not see nor encounter these paranormal creatures but the Orang Asli do, possibly because they are attuned to the spiritual world. The worst sin in Orang Asli culture is to show disrespect to the unseen inhabitants of the forest by talking loudly or singing. One must always respect the many spirits that dwell in the trees, thickets, pools and caves. They are especially wary of the government's mad rush to clear the primary forest and replace it with palm oil plantations. They say the resulting impact on biodiversity will be profound and calamitous and that it is based on a false economic policy.

On a recent visit to Carey Island, I was invited to attend a traditional Mah Meri wedding. That particular village is famous for two things- fresh seafood and superb masks carved out of wood by the Mah Meri of Kampung Sungai Bumbun. In some respects, it was similar to a Malay wedding. The happy bride and groom sat on the bridal couch and were sprinkled with yellow rice and scented water by the villagers. The pair exchanged marriage vows before a Catholic priest, Fr. Manos Pereira and the village headman. The family members, relatives and guests embraced the pair as a sign of blessing. We all sat down to a sumptuous wedding feast. We were served with a mountain of exotic food including the favourite dishes of the tribe – rendang cooked with monkey, pangolin and wild boar. Finally, there was music and dancing, much fun and merriment. There was a plentiful supply of beer, rice wine and peach brandy. During the celebrations, the visiting priest told me a most extraordinary story. It happened not in Carey Island but further south in the Orang Asli village, Kampung Sebir, beyond Seremban.

One day, Tok Dongkok's two sons, Saul and Jonas were cutting tiger grass and packing it in tidy bundles for the women folk in the village to make into brooms which the Orang Asli sold in the village market and in the towns in the Klang Valley and along the coast. One of the things that the visitor notices in every Malay house is the ubiquitous broom. It is used to sweep floors and courtyards. It is also used to sweep up the litter in shopping centres, food halls, hotel lobbies and public places. It is quite useless as a floor cleaner since it does not suck up fine dust like a hoover but it is effective in removing surface litter such as paper, cigarette ends, dead cockroaches and orange peel which Malays scatter about in great profusion. Some Malaysians have not yet come to terms with the rubbish bin and they see no reason to dispose of rubbish when an army of cleaning ladies will do the job anyhow.

'Thank God the Malays are a dirty race,' Tok Dongkok, the village headman, once remarked because he knew that they needed his people to keep their homes and towns clean and tidy. Furthermore, he knew that waste material had a certain value and could be recycled. The Orang Asli would travel from town to town each day, collecting bags of garbage, the contents of which they sorted into plastics, tin, bottles, paper and metal. The waste material was then sold by weight to a recycling plant in Seremban.

The Orang Asli are extremely industrious and make up to 50 brooms each day as well as a range of rattan baskets and prayer mats which fetch good prices in the central markets across the state. In fact, their intricate basketry sells like hot cakes, providing much needed income for the Orang Asli community. Most Malay households normally have two or three amahs, constantly sweeping the rooms and yards but, of course, a broom has a short life span and people would buy not one but six brooms at a time. One might imagine that with the advent of technology, the days of the broom were numbered but that is not so. I lived in a large condominium in Subang Jaya and every day an army of cleaning ladies sweep the corridors and public areas with brooms.

In recent years, the Orang Asli and Mah Meri have developed several cottage industries, thanks to a government scheme. One such industry is organic farming for the production of fruits and vegetables as well as free-range poultry and eggs. Hence, although far from being well off, the village people are much better off than previously and all the income is pooled and shared among the community.

In Kampung Sebir, as in other Orang Asli areas, there was a certain amount of harassment of the village people by the state authorities. Their rightful traditional land was being taken away from them and their basic human rights were ignored. The river Koyan flows through the village and on the north side there are neat rows of new houses, a clinic, a mosque, a primary school and a few government offices. However, in order to gain access to those modern homes and amenities, one had 'to cross the river', that is, become a Muslim. The vast majority of the Orang Asli refused to abandon their traditional animist beliefs. They seemed to prefer to live in their squalid thatched huts and send their children to the local Mission school. They are a happy people and live in close harmony with nature. But all of that is by the way.

One day, on the left side of the river, Saul and Jonas had cleared a large patch of tiger grass with their bill hooks. They were about to return to the village at midday when they noticed a moving object in the long grass. They froze in their tracks when, through the long green stalks, they saw the bronze and green patchwork body of a hooded king cobra[3] heading towards the river. Of all the creatures in the rainforest, the hooded king cobra is the most revered. This is hardly surprising since, like the tiger, it has a body of stunning beauty and symmetry. In Orang Asli lore, the king cobra was the first creature to inhabit the earth. It was regarded as the progenitor of all life and the source of all fecundity. One particular hooded king cobra, known as Abu Ong, inhabited their ancestral land and was accorded the status of a god. He had cosmic powers within the domain of the rainforest. There were many epic tales about the deeds of Abu Ong. He was also honoured in song and dance. One of the latest tales you may be told is called 'The Snake Rises'. It tells the tale of an unfortunate attempt to kill Abu Ong and how he rose from the dead, in a manner of speaking. This is how it happened.

On seeing the moving object in the long grass, Saul and Jonas struck without delay. They rained blows on the cobra's head, stunning it instantly. Then, they wrapped it in a gunny sack and carried it back to the village on a stout pole. There was great excitement in the village as the two men appeared bearing the giant snake. It was placed in a large metal pot while family members collected all the ingredients needed to make snake stew. It would then be left to simmer in the huge pot over a fire of charcoal.

Everything was going according to plan and Tok Dongkok sharpened his parang to chop the cobra into 2-inch-wide chunks but no sooner had he lifted the lid of the pot than a cloud of steam arose and filled the room. To everyone's amazement, the king cobra sprang out, twirled several times in the air, darted across the floor between Tok Dongkok's legs and scurried into the lallang (long grass). Clearly, this was no ordinary snake but the revered snake god, Abu Ong.

News of the cobra's capture and its subsequent dramatic escape soon spread and people came from the neighbouring villages to pay their respects to Abu Ong. They offered lotus flowers, duck's eggs and pigs' liver to appease the sacred cobra. They knew it was vital to track down Abu Ong and beg his pardon for the grave wrong done to him before he exacted retribution from the village. They did not have far to go. There was a knoll overlooking the river and on it were several mango trees. The villagers spotted the metallic bronze body of Abu Ong in one of the trees. He emerged every now and then from the foliage. He raised the anterior portion of his body, showing his fangs and hissing loudly. Then a great hush came over crowd and Tok Dongkok addressed the sacred cobra: 'Great lord and master, know that we the Orang Asli people profoundly regret the events of this day and the great dishonor shown to you. I beg to inform you that it was all a terrible mistake on our part and we beseech you to pardon our tragic misdeed.'

As he spoke, Abu Ong emerged from behind the topmost branch, his lower body coiled around the tree trunk and his upper body raised aloft. His head swayed to and fro, his magnificent hood quivering menacingly. A loud hissing sound rent the air and an orange glow appeared about Abu Ong. His body shone with a luminous green and bronze colour. It was a dazzling sight-the kind of magic vision that one reads about in olden legends. The villagers rubbed their eyes in disbelief and were struck with fear and awe. At last, Abu Ong spoke in a high-pitched voice: 'Some people act in ignorance and that is excusable but others are driven by greed. We must stand together to protect the integrity of the forest. You must know that Abu Ong will never harm the people of the forest.'

Then the mango tree shook violently as if in a gale and its fruit rained down onto the grass below. Finally, Abu Ong disappeared in a cloud of mist, leaving the crowd speechless. The villagers quietly gathered up the fruit and returned to the village. To their utter astonishment, in each hut, they found a basket of choice foods – Abu Ong's parting gift to the Orang Asli community. To this day, that mango tree in Kampung Sebir is revered by the Orang Asli. Should you visit Kampung Sebir, you can see the mango tree where Abu Ong appeared and the older villagers will tell you that he addressed them not in Malay but in their Asli dialect. That tree still bears the best fruit in the village and is much sought after in memory of Abu Ong.

Recently, I was informed that a missionary priest, Fr. Pereira, who worked among the Orang Asli in Negeri Sembilan, had made a study of the snakes in that state and recorded some of the folklore associated with them. In his paper 'Snakes as Spirits' (1922), there is a poem in praise of Abu Ong, which rendered in English, is as follows:

My name is Abu Ong.
I'm a cobra brown and long.
My home is in the mango tree
My kingdom all the forest free.

I am no common slitty mover
No puffing adder, no saw-scaled viper.
I am the protector of our land
Now being stolen by an unseen hand.

I am not your biblical foe
Spreading evil, grief and woe.
The kiss of death is but for those
Whose evil deeds I shall expose.

ENDNOTES:

1   *Orang Asli*: The indigenous people and the oldest inhabitants of Peninsular Malaysia. There are three main Orang Asli tribes – the Semang (or Negrito) in the northern highlands, the Senoi in the central region and the Proto-Malay in the Southern region. They live in remote forest areas, in stilt houses, often beside a river. They speak various Orang Asli dialects and most of them also speak Malay. They are very poor; it is estimated that 80% of all Orang Asli live below the poverty line. For more on the Orang Asli, see Moore, W. & Cubitt, G. 2000. *This is Malaysia*. London: New Holland Publishers.

2   *hantu*: spirits or ghosts that dwell in the forest, rivers, lakes and hide in old tree trunks, caves and in the jungle undergrowth. They are different from the spirits of Hindu folklore in that they belong to animism which attributes a living soul to plants, inanimate objects and natural phenomena.

3   *hooded king cobra*: The largest venomous snake in the world. It can grow to 5.5 metres long. Its venom can kill an elephant. It can spit into its prey's eyes. Cobra meat is much sought after across Southeast Asia and especially in Thailand.

9

SIX DJINN IN A JAR

The djinn[1] are free spirits which one associates with Arabia and they came to Malaysia with the advent of Islam. Unlike other hantu (spirits), the djinn are mentioned in the Qur'an. There is a surah [2] entitled *Surat al-Jinn*. According to the Qur'an, the djinn are made of smokeless flame or 'the fire of the scorching wind'. They appear in various forms. Some have wings and fly in the air; others take the form of a snake or vulture, while yet others appear as a tall man in a white garb. The djinn differ from other hantu in two respects – they are male and very dangerous. If they attack, they can eat a person's heart (Lim,[3] 2008: 40). Of all hantu, they are the most difficult to cast out. Like humans, they have free will and can be good or evil but djinn stories are normally about the evil ones. They seem to vary along a scale of malevolence from the slightly annoying to the demonic. That is why some people believe they are fallen angels, doing Satan's work on earth but that view is not found in the Qur'an.

Among the Taman tribe in Borneo, the djinn are regarded a 'hill ghosts', living in the forest or hills (Lim, 2008: 46). The Borneo djinn are more dangerous and grotesque than their counterpart on the Peninsula. They live in the forest and may be seen on the tops of trees. They have only one eye which is red. They take the form of a bald bare-chested wrestler with a pony tail, a massive chest like a barrel and huge arms like tree trunks.

According to reports in the Malay press, the djinn are still active in many parts of Malaysia. They often hide in schools and public buildings and abduct teenage girls. They cause mass hysteria, panic and pandemonium and they are the bane of every headmistress. The problem is that they are very difficult to locate and banish. They may hide in a vase, or an egg, or a biscuit tin. Only a skilled bomoh[4] can track them down, capture them and remove them in a special container. Most djinn are extremely mischievous and only a few bomohs[4] know how to neutralise them. They are a constant threat to young Muslims and sometimes take possession of teenage girls. It is believed that they can be frightened off by the Qur'an but this is not so, since they are able to read the holy book. Their mission seems to be to confuse Muslims, disrupt normal life and generally create mischief and mayhem. It is said that they sometimes clash with the angels, resulting in violent thunder storms when the two forces collide. The mere sight of a djinn may prevent hens laying their eggs or cows giving milk. They can even cause a child to be stillborn. The djinn seem to be forever up to mischief. They are known to swoop on late-night travellers in the Klang Valley and throw them into the muddy river or storm drains. They like to vandalise property and disrupt systems, for instance, by throwing logs onto the railway tracks. They are believed to be behind the mysterious disappearance of teenage girls who are subsequently discovered in odd places such as a graveyard, a laundry van or inside a cement mixer.

A number of teenage girls were reported to have vanished several times in Johor Bahru and were later found in odd places, in a semi-conscious state, unable to remember what had happened and acting in a manner that suggested they might be possessed by an evil spirit. Bomohs often warned young people not to mess with the djinn. They pointed out that a djinn often hid inside an egg and they advised people not to pick up an egg should they find one after sunset on a path, in a discarded box or under a bush.

During a visit to Johor Bahru, I came across an Englishman who was collecting material for a book which he intended to have published in Singapore under the title 'The Other Malaysia'. His name was Sandy Beresford and he was something of an expert on the paranormal. He had documented many instances of ghostly apparitions, tribal beliefs about spirits and cases of demonic possession. Seldom have I met a man so absorbed in his chosen field. Much of his data was obtained from bomohs and he showed me photographs of various people who claimed to have had ghostly experiences. He was one of those people who had the rare gift of engaging you totally in a fascinating tale of personal experiences and wanderings across Borneo and the Malay Peninsula. Unfortunately, his book was never published because he died in tragic circumstances some time later. He was gored to death by a wild boar on a banana plantation. I still recall one of the many stories he told me about the djinn. He told me that he had been in Sabah recently and while hill walking in the Crocker Range near the village of Donggongon he met a bomoh, Tok Batin, who warned him not to go near a certain thicket of mango trees in the valley below. He said that several djinn were hiding there. Sandy asked him if djinn were real or just a myth to attract tourists to certain remote places in Sabah, just like fairies in Ireland.

'Tuan Sandy,' he said 'they are real all right. Sure, amn't I tormented by them.' He then sprinkled Sandy with holy water from the gereja [5] in Donggongon to ward off the evil ones. So, it appears that the djinn target Christians as well as Muslims. That was a new finding for Dr. Beresford because all the djinn literature spoke of djinn only in the context of Islamic culture.

Haji Omar Metali lived in Kampung Sungai Rengit, a quiet fishing village overlooking the sea in Johore. Most of the young people there now work in Johor Bahru which has become a major industrial and commercial city. The main activity in the village used to be fishing but that has declined due to diminishing fish stocks. Haji Omar was a fisherman and he had a teenage daughter, Siti Noor who was a bit on the wild side. She was a good Muslim but she used to frequent what her parents called 'unhealthy places' in Johor Bahru along with her motorbike friends. She was friendly and vivacious, into pop music and heavy metal. She also smoked cigarettes which is not common among Muslim women. Her mother often complained that Siti Noor dressed provocatively in that while she always wore the tudong[6] on formal occasions, she also wore skin-tight jeans, skimpy tops and a baseball cap when mixing with the 'mods'. Like many Muslim girls in Malaysia, she was torn between Islamic mores and the norms of a permissive society. However, Haji Omar loved her dearly because he knew that she had strong Islamic principles and would never engage in 'haram' activities such as smoking the weed or drinking alcohol.

Prior to my visit to Johor, Siti Noor became the talk of the kampung when she suddenly vanished on several occasions only to be found a day or two later in odd locations such as the local cemetery or a fishing boat or a shoe factory. On her return home, she would spend several days in a daze before reverting to her normal self. When asked to explain her mysterious disappearance, Siti Noor was at a loss. All she could say was that her mind went blank and that she had no memory of being abducted or molested. The police suspected that the Mat Rempit [7] were up to their tricks but there was no evidence to link Siti Noor's disappearance to them.

Haji Omar was a worried man. He suspected that the djinn were involved in his daughter's vanishing act. Accordingly, he asked the local bomoh to come and investigate the matter. The bomoh spoke with Siti Noor and he fumigated the whole house but he found no traces of a djinn. Several bomohs also offered their services for free after reading about Siti Noor's plight in the newspapers. They prayed, recited verses from the Qur'an and gave Siti Noor some zam zam[8] to drink but all to no avail. Siti Noor's vanishings continued and each time she was found in the most unlikely places. On her return home, she looked listless and spent a day or two in bed recovering from her ordeal. Why the djinn picked on Siti Noor is impossible to say. Some said she was 'wayward' and the djinn were merely trying to remind her of her Islamic obligations. Others took the view that the djinn were a bad lot and randomly abducted young females out of spite and ill will.

Then one day Haji Omar managed to contact Abdul Hakim, a very famous bomoh in Johor. He was a specialist in exorcism and the capture of djinn. He seemed quite confident that he would be successful where others had failed. He arrived in Kampung Sungai Rengit one Friday afternoon and proceeded to Haji Omar's house where he found Siti Noor lying on a mattress on the floor in a trance-like state. Abdul Hakim knew at once that it was a case of djinn possession and that he would have to conduct an exorcism ritual to drive out the evil spirit. He recited verses from the Qur'an, then touching Siti Noor lightly on the forehead he addressed the djinn: 'Spirit of darkness, I hereby command you in the name of Allah the most merciful to come out of the temple which you inhabit – the body of Siti Noor.'

As soon as he said those words, Siti Noor's eyes went white and began to rotate in their sockets. While Abdul Hakim bent over Siti Noor, her whole body convulsed in orgasmic shrieks. Foaming at the mouth, she screamed the vilest abuse at Abdul Kakim. 'Don't touch me, you fornicator, you son of Satan. Your hands are unclean and your mind is full of lust.' The tension in the room was unbearable. Then, Siti Noor's mouth opened wide and out flew a winged serpent. It circled the room several times screeching and spitting fire. Eventually, the flying djinn came to rest on a shelf and Abdul Hakim seized it with his snake thongs.[9] He deposited the djinn in a large jar and it immediately transformed into an egg. The people waited with bated breath, too terrified to utter a word. Then, raising his eyes to heaven, Abdul Hakim repeated the same injunction to the spirit of darkness and once more out flew another djinn in the form of a winged serpent. It too flew about in a demented rage before coming to rest on the kitchen table. Quick as lightening, Abdul Hakim captured it and deposited it in the jar, whereupon it too changed into an egg. In like manner, Ahmad Hakim ejected a total of six djinn, all of which were imprisoned in the jar.

At last, peace descended upon Siti Noor. She sat up and rubbing her eyes, asked: 'Who are all these people? Am I dead or what?' Abdul Kakim assured her: 'My dear, you are very much alive. We must all thank Allah for your deliverance.' There was much rejoicing in the family and in the kampung. The jar with the six djinn in it was sealed and thrown into the sea and that was the last time that the people of Kampung Sungai Rengit were troubled by the djinn. At last, Haji Omar's life returned to normal and he was much relieved that the djinn responsible for spiriting his daughter away had been captured and banished.

If you go to Kampung Sungai Rengit, the local people will show you a knoll which was the favourite haunt of the djinn in the olden times. But fear not, the djinn there have been banished by Abdul Hakim.

Endnotes:

1   *djinn*: sometimes spelt *jinn* are fire spirits, capable of good but usually portrayed as wicked. (McLoughlin, S. 2007. *World Religions.* London: Star Fire.)
2   *surah:* A verse in the Quran.
3   *Danny Lim* (2008). *The Malaysian Book of the Undead.* Kuala Lumpur: Mata Hari Books

4   *bomoh*: The 'spirit doctor' or traditional medicine-man in Malay culture. He performs rituals to placate the hantu and he can cleanse a village of malignant spirits. For more on the bomoh, see Danny Lim (2008) above, pp 16-21.

5   *gereja*: The Malay word for church, from the Portuguese 'igreja'.

6   *tudong*: Malay word for headscarf; it conceals the hair but not the face.

7   *Mat Rempit*: Street gangs and snatch thieves on motorcycles that hang about in Kuala Lumpur, engaged in anti-social behaviour.

8   *zam zam*: holy water from the Zam Zam well in Mecca

9   *snake thongs*: A steel rod at the top of which is a jaw-like mechanism the opens and closes by pressing a lever. It is part of the tool kit of snake hunters.

A COVERT AFFAIR

Rupert Orr came from a long line of Orrs in Dungannon, Northern Ireland. The family, being Planter stock, had been granted a vast estate east of Dungannon, on the shores of Lough Neagh. They had prospered in spite of sporadic civil strife and became major players in the linen industry which made the province famous. The Orrs were staunch Protestants and had their own chapel on the estate. However, they were not as bigoted as many of their Orange Order[1] countrymen partly because the male Orrs were all educated at Trinity College Dublin where religious bigotry was frowned upon and where one received a liberal education.

Rupert, unlike his two brothers, had little interest in the cultivation, preparation and spinning of flax, much less in farming and flour milling. He loved hunting, fishing and riding his pet pony Bones around the estate. He was a keen angler and he would spend hours teaching the sons and daughters of the landed gentry the art of fly fishing. He was much admired for his ready wit and ebullient conversation. He was, in many respects, the antithesis of the dour Ulster Presbyterian. He was jolly and carefree, not especially religious and had no interest in the schizoid world of the Orange Order. He was something of a naturalist and had a passion for country pursuits. He spent hours every day reading. He devoured books and was most impressed not only by the great Victorian novelists but by modern writers like James Joyce. He had read *Ulysses*;[2] knew its geography and its unique Dublin voices from his own experience of life in that city. He tried to persuade his father to read the book. It seems that the elder Orr did so most reluctantly and his verdict was that it was 'incomprehensible and hardly worth the effort of reading it.' He hoped that the book would remain forever banned in Northern Ireland and the UK.

Not having a great deal of interest in farming or helping to run the estate, which in any case was destined to become his elder brother's property, Rupert decided to enlist in the British Colonial Service and eventually was posted to India. He loved India, which in those days, in the early 30s, was the jewel in the crown of the British Empire. As a commercial officer in Government House in Poona, his duties were far from demanding. He was involved mostly in rural development schemes because the Raj[3] thought it proper to show concern for the betterment of rural farmers, forestry workers and plantation staff. He soon learned a great deal about the management of large tea and rubber plantations. The Resident of Bombay, Clive Templeton, was well pleased with Rupert's efforts to boost three of India's major exports-tea, rubber and jute.

During long leave, Rupert did not return home to Ulster but spent some time in the government hill station in Poona. For a minimal sum, he enjoyed the best of Indian cuisine and spent many happy hours in the British Club where he soon became quite expert at colonial pursuits – bridge, billiards and bagatelle. He took up polo at weekends and he loved the sport. He also made the acquaintance of the Maharajah of Jaipur. His Highness liked Rupert and invited him to stay at his palace, a massive Moorish edifice overlooking a lake. The Maharajah was an Oxford graduate and a consummate cricketer. It was the Maharajah who introduced Rupert to polo and philately, a hobby that fascinated many an Indian prince. When he was leaving Jaipur, the Maharajah presented Rupert with an album of rare Rajasthan postage stamps, which would nowadays fetch a small fortune on the stamp market.

Rupert's prize possession, however, was his automobile – a superb Bugatti coupe. Few cars have been created with the elegance of the Bugatti. Among its many special features were cloth seats and a four-panelled sunroof. It was dark maroon with green trim and a hardwood dashboard. Even the Maharajah of Jaipur, who was no stranger to luxury, had never seen such a gem of a car. When Rupert turned up at the polo grounds or the cricket club in his brand-new Bugatti, heads turned. It had cost a small fortune even in the 1930s, but Rupert could well afford it because after the demise of his father, he received his share of the inheritance, a sum of £15,000 (Today, £800,000). Rupert was not a vain man but he simply loved beautiful objects, be they cars, Persian carpets, horses, vintage postage stamps or rare books. Naturally, he was a big hit with the ladies and he had several torrid affairs with sundry British ladies of the upper class. It was rumoured that every good-looking lady in Poona and Bombay, whether single or married, had slept with Rupert. The truth of the matter was that he was far more attracted to the tall, slim, dark-skinned Indian women who worked as clerks and cleaners in Government House but of course any dalliance with an Indian woman would have been unthinkable in those days.

Then, one day, Rupert decided that he had sufficient capital to invest in a money-making enterprise, so he resigned from government service, left India and made his way to the Federated Malay States with a view to establishing a rubber plantation. Malacca was the cradle of the rubber industry and rubber was one of Malaysia's main exports. At that time, in the early 30s, rubber had replaced coffee and tapioca as the dominant crop in Malacca and Johor. Most of the rubber plantations were concentrated in the western coastal plain. Chinese and Indian money lenders provided the capital to clear the forest and plant rubber trees. Rupert had acquired a good knowledge of rubber production during his sojourn in India and he purchased a small estate near Bukit Lintang, about six miles inland from Malacca city. It was a risky undertaking as rubber trees require a gestation period of six years and great supervision is needed to ensure that the saplings are properly nurtured to maturity. His work force were all Tamils from Southern India and Ceylon and only a man of means like Rupert had the financial resources to pay, feed and provide rudimentary welfare for the Indian migrants who were housed on the estate. Unlike many other plantation owners, Rupert believed that the labourer was worthy of his hire and workers were paid a good wage, plus an annual bonus. Moreover, he won the loyalty of the Tamil workers, who always referred to him as Sir Rupert.

Meanwhile, further north, at Ayer Molek, Frank Hennessey had established a stud farm and racing stables, called 'Forest Hill'. Frank had grown up in the bloodstock trade in Ireland and there was nothing about horses and horse racing that he did not know. In the enclosure at the racecourse, Frank Hennessey stood out. He was a man of enormous physical presence. He was a good six foot tall and as stout as a village parson. His sleek ginger hair and beard gave him a wealthy and well-groomed appearance. He was a big man with a big heart and even though he had spent years living abroad, he still retained an Irish accent and an Irish temper. He was not a man to trifle with. He was well known among the planter community in Malacca and no party would be complete without Frank and his delightful wife, Estelle de Santos, a raven-haired lady with a Latin temperament and the grace and beauty of the Portuguese Eurasian. Like Frank, Estelle was a Roman Catholic. She came from a wealthy family of wine merchants in Malacca.

In those days, the rubber planters enjoyed a rich social life. There was an endless stream of parties. Hardly a week went by without some celebration or 'fiesta'. The major players were the British but the rich man's club also included Indian businessmen, Chinese traders, Malay nobles and Portuguese Eurasians. For colonial settlers, it was the best of times, in a land of great natural beauty and cheap labour. Rupert, like the other rubber barons, held an annual ball and it was a splendid affair. His wooded estate and impressive colonial mansion provided the perfect setting for a lavish bash. He was one of the few eligible bachelors in the region and there was much speculation as to which of the beautiful ladies would win his hand. There was no shortage of beautiful women. The only problem for Rupert was that few of them were Protestant; most were Hindu, or Buddhist, or worse still, Roman Catholic. Besides, he preferred the slim oriental woman to the plump red-cheeked English rose. Everyone looked forward to Rupert's ball and it was a spectacular success. All the guests had a good time, none more so than Estelle, who was the belle of the ball.

In the days and weeks following the ball, Rupert became infatuated with Estelle and she offered to help him with interior design and period furnishing. Not surprisingly, a warm relationship soon developed between the pair. It is not always easy to say which factors push a married woman into the arms of the single man. It may the thrill of the chase or it may be the fact that a forbidden relationship makes it all the more exciting. It was probably the case that Estelle felt neglected by her husband both emotionally and physically. She craved the attention that Rupert gave her and as long as Frank never found out, why shouldn't she and Rupert enjoy an intimate relationship?

However, one evening, Rupert's foreman, Adam Grant, happened to pass by the bay window at the side of the house. He often called after dinner to discuss plantation matters with Rupert over a glass of whisky. Knowing that Estellle was a frequent visitor, he peered through the window to ensure that the coast was clear before ringing the doorbell. He was totally unprepared for what he saw. Rupert was sitting on a chair, semi-naked, his back to the window. Estelle was perched above him on the mahogany table, in a black chiffon negligee, her bare legs wrapped about Rupert's head. Both were laughing and sipping wine or champagne. Adam could hear the metallic crackling sounds of a gramophone drifting across the room.

Adam did not loiter a second longer. He knew that Rupert and Estelle were good friends but he had no idea that they were lovers. He dashed to his apartment at the rear of the mansion and poured himself a large scotch. What was he to do about this unholy revelation? He dare not tell Frank because to do so would almost certainly result in blood on the carpet. He could imagine Frank in a wild rage bursting in, shotgun at the ready, about to shoot both lovers at point blank range. Such an outcome had to be avoided at all costs. It would be unseemly to disrupt the harmony of the plantation community. In the end, Adam decided that it was in everyone's best interest to say nothing. After all, he concluded, most things happen for a reason. And so, the covert affair went on and nobody was the wiser.

Rupert and Frank remained the best of friends and each prospered in the good life of colonial Malaya. As for Estelle, she kept her candle burning at both ends. The only one who was shocked and scandalised by the clandestine affair was the foreman, Grant. He came to the understanding that a woman can be both dutiful wife and scheming whore. But then who was he, a humble foreman, to penetrate the mysteries of the female mind?

ENDNOTES:

1   *Orange Order:* A Protestant political society in Northern Ireland for the defence of Protestantism and the Union with Great Britain.
2   *Ulysses:* The famous novel by James Joyce about a day in the life of Leopold Bloom.
3   *Raj*: British rule in India.

11

A MAN OF WAR

When George Bernard Collins looked in the mirror, he did not like what he saw. He was in his mid-fifties but be looked like a man in his mid-seventies. He was as grey as a badger and his pallid skin was gnarled like an old oak. Some of the damage could no doubt be attributed to a long army career in the tropical jungles of Southeast Asia. F. Spencer Chapman,[1] whose heroic campaign against the Japanese in the Malayan jungle in World War 2 is well known, attributed his survival to the basic rule that 'the jungle is neutral'. As a lone operator behind enemy lines, one had to be a survivalist, expecting nothing and accepting the dangers and bounty of the jungle in equal measure. The jungle exacted a high price on all who took refuge in it. It was especially hard on the Caucasian body which is ill-equipped for the rigours of life in the rainforest. However, GB, as his friends called him, had to admit that in his case most of the damage was self-inflicted. He had smoked all his life and after being demobilised in 1946, he hit the bottle in real earnest and drank enough vodka to sink a battleship. Still, he was alive, somewhat battered by a life that would have caused a man of lesser resolve to jump off a cliff.

'It's important to stay alive,' he'd say to himself. Only a military man would say such a thing. GB had had his fair share of brushes with death in the Malayan jungle, both during the Pacific war and later as a member of the British Special Forces in Malaysia. It was ironic too. GB had done his bit for King and country but his grandparents who were Irish settled in Manchester and remained staunch republicans all their lives. They did not support the IRA but they were not surprised that quite a few Irish people living in the UK did.

Now, looking back over twenty years of active service in the British Army, GB could recall every detail of the two great wars that had dominated his life-the Battle of Borneo (1942-45) and the Malayan Emergency (1948-60). In 1940, he and a company of Royal Marines had been dispatched to Malaya to prepare for a possible Japanese naval invasion. They set up the British Operations Centre at Tanjung Pengelih in Johor, on a hill behind the Immigration and Customs checkpoint. It was a massive military complex, including an underground hospital, barracks, tunnels, a command post, naval guns and anti-aircraft installations. However, the Japanese did not come from the sea. The Pacific War commenced with the invasion of Kota Bahru in Kelantan in December 1941. Within two months, the Japanese had captured Peninsular Malaya. Then they invaded North Borneo, landing near Miri in Sarawak.

During the Japanese occupation, various guerrilla forces battled the enemy from the jungles of Malaya. The Battle of Borneo (1942-45) was a dirty war. The Japanese high command embarked on a reign of terror. With unspeakable cruelty and frequent reprisals against ethnic Chinese, they annexed much of North Borneo. Meanwhile, the tide was beginning to turn against the Japanese on the mainland. The British Army knew a thing or two about jungle warfare and made good use of Iban trackers to uncover Japanese commandoes in the jungle. Then the Royal Marines moved in and cut them off.

GB used to say that he did not have a 'big' war – mostly routine stuff, escorting convoys and taking part in mopping up operations. The heavy fighting was in Borneo where the Commonwealth army forced the Japanese to surrender. The war ended with the surrender of the Japanese 37th Army by Lt. Gen. Baba Masao on Labuan on 10th September 1945. However, victory was not achieved cheaply, as the rows of war graves in Labuan attest.

Hardly had one war ended when a new war erupted. The Malayan Emergency[2] was a guerrilla war fought from 1948 – 60 between the British and the Malayan National Liberation Army (MNLA), the military wing of the Malayan Communist Party. Malaya was badly shaken by the Japanese occupation and when the war ended, the economy was in poor shape.

There was unemployment, low wages and food shortages, all of which sparked street protests and unrest orchestrated by the Communist Party. The British responded in the usual manner by introducing emergency measures to quell the uprising. The MNLA was outlawed and the police were given power to imprison communists and their allies without trial. The MNLA, led by Chin Peng,[3] retreated to the rural areas and used guerrilla tactics. They were supported by the Chinese who had been denied equal rights and were very poor. Initially, the insurgents seemed to be gaining the upper hand. They sabotaged installations, derailed trains, burnt rubber plantations and generated civil unrest. They also conducted military strikes against the British and Malayan security forces in the form of ambushes. All of this narrative one can find in history books but my version came direct from the mouth of GB who had been there in the thick of the battle.

The aim of the British was to win the 'hearts and minds' of the Malays and to put pressure on the MNLA by patrolling the jungle. GB was assigned to a company of Special Forces to track down the communists in the Selangor jungle. Other British platoons were also involved, in particular the Scots Guards. They operated like commandos behind enemy lines and were involved in many armed encounters with the communists. GB and his men found life in the jungle very tough but they were greatly assisted by Iban trackers who were employed to carry out surveillance.

Inevitably, in war, dreadful things happen. GB was shocked and sickened by the Batang Kali[4] massacre which took place in December 1948. A platoon of the Scots Guards surrounded a rubber estate at Batang Kali, Selangor and shot 24 unarmed men in the back before setting fire to the village. As a professional soldier, GB was outraged at this atrocity and he was even more outraged when the Colonial Attorney General exonerated the Scots Guards of any wrongdoing because he believed that mass executions would deter insurgents. Years later, some of the Scots Guards involved in the shooting confessed to the crime but the British government steadfastly refused to re-open the case and correct the record.

Eventually, the MNLA was defeated and Chin Peng fled to China. During the conflict, the security forces killed 6,700 MNLA guerrillas. It was a major blow for communism in Southeast Asia. GB retired from army life with two war medals and a modest war pension. After the war, he retired to Port Dixon where he invested in a small bar. That was probably not a very astute move by a man with a drink problem. It was a small English type pub with a steady stream of regulars who enjoyed GB's seemingly endless war stories. He never appeared drunk but he had a dozen shots of Russian vodka every day and it showed. There were days when he was legless and he would sleep on a foam mattress on the floor behind the bar. His Filipina assistant, known locally as Judy of the Big Boobs, ran the show, but things went from bad to worse and GB looked like a dead man walking.

Whenever I visited Port Dixon, I would stop off for a chat with GB. He told me he had decided to stay on in Malaysia because he knew he would not fit into the new Britain that had emerged in the post-war years. According the GB, Britain had become a multicultural, multiracial society. It had lost its identity and its soul. The cream of the crop had perished in the two World Wars. What really annoyed him was that he and his comrades in the British Army had spent twenty years or more in defence of the realm, British values and the British way of life, only to discover that the whole demographic landscape had changed beyond recognition. Britain was no longer 'great' in any sense. It was just a ragbag of subcultures – a peripheral and unwilling member of the European Union. He was not at all racist. His only contention was that a nation should cherish and preserve its culture, language, identity and dignity. Britain had to concede independence to the colonies but it should have retained all of its strategic bases east of Suez. Naturally, his strong views provoked a lot of heated discussion and I suspect that was exactly what GB wanted. He'd say the most outrageous things, for instance, he'd say that the British had gone soft in the head and that the government in Westminster was 'a ship of fools'.

In quiet moments, GB was a different man. He was a sensitive soul and generous to a fault. He told me that the war still haunted him and he'd wake up at night to the rat-tat-tat of machine gun fire. He was part of the British war machine but he was troubled by the concept of 'justifiable war'. In what sense was the jungle campaign against the communists justifiable, he would ask himself. He knew that war was based on the 'law of talons' – an eye for an eye etc. He personally had no compunction in killing Japanese troops during the war in Malaya. They were an ungodly lot, who crossed the line of common decency. But the same could not be said about Chin Peng and the communists. They were fighting a war of liberation and did not kill for the sake of killing. As a Christian, he recited the Lord's Prayer every day. 'Forgive us our trespasses as we forgive those who trespass against us.' That archaic word 'trespass' implied that some people would cross the line, invade our territory and deny our human rights. At his Grammar School in Manchester, the Christian Brothers had asserted that human life was sacred. 'Thou shat not kill.' But the army chaplain had explained that as long as they operated within the ambit of the Geneva Convention, killing was lawful. His mission as a soldier was to kill the enemy. Still, he was horrified by the Batang Kali massacre. That particular incident had sullied the good reputation of the British Army which, unlike the Japanese, observed the Geneva Convention regarding the conduct of war.

During my last visit to Port Dixon, I heard that there had been a major confrontation between GB and his woman Judy. It happened after his return from the annual World War 2 commemoration at the War Memorial in Labuan. A 'Remembrance Day' is held every November at the War Cemetery to honour the 4,000 Australian, New Zealand and British Allied servicemen who lost their lives in the Battle of Borneo. GB used to look forward to meeting many of his old comrades in arms, all wearing their war medals proudly, as war veterans are entitled to do. However, when he returned to Port Dixon a week later, he found the till empty and stocks low. Judy had no explanation. There ensued a bitter exchange of words, during which Judy hit GB over the head with a vodka bottle, concussing the poor man. Not content with having delivered a knock-out blow, she then beat him senseless with a broom handle. She would probably have killed him there and then but for the intervention of two sailors who happened to call. GB was rushed to hospital bleeding profusely. It was reported that he was in Intensive Care and his regular customers stated collecting drift wood for a funeral pyre on the beach. However, to everyone's amazement, GB somehow survived. A week later, he was back behind the bar, his head bandaged and his left arm in a sling. Needless to say, that was the end of his partnership with Judy. He admitted that the battering he had received at her hands was worse than all the tribulations he had endured in his army career. A local artist did a series of cartoons of the incident, called 'The Punch and Judy Show' and these were displayed on the wall.

I have no idea what happened to GB. Some say he sold out and went to the Philippines with another Filipina woman. I suspect that the bottle finally took its toll. He once told me that his inners had been shot, not by sniper fire, but by the demon drink. I think a fitting epitaph for GB would read: 'Old soldiers never die; they just fade away'.

ENDNOTES:

1   *F. Spencer Chapman*, author of 'The Jungle is Neutral', (1949). Lyon Press. A classic account of the World War 2 in the Malayan jungle by the great bird-watching war hero. For over 3 years, he blew up trains, bridges and Japanese troops in the jungles of Malaya.
2   *The Malayan Emergency*: The guerrilla war in the Malay jungles between the British Colonial Forces and the Communists under Chin Peng 1948-1960. See Barbar, N. (1971), *War of the Running Dogs*. London: Collins.
3   *Chin Peng*: The Communist guerrilla leader who caused the Malayan Emergency in 1948.
4   *Batang Kali*: 'Britain's My Lai massacre'. On December 12th, 1948, the 7th Platoon, G Company of the Scots Guards surrounded a rubber estate at Batang Kali in Selangor and shot 24 men before setting fire to the village. See *Slaughter and Deception at Batang Kali*, (2009). Ian Ward and Norma Miraflor. Singapore: Media Masters.

A MATTER OF HISTORY

Oliver Tan grew up on the island of Penang, 'Pearl of the Orient'. Although he was Chinese, he did not speak a word of that language. His mother tongue was English. His culture was English. He was educated at St. Xavier's Institution in George Town and Nottingham University. He read law at university and loved the subject. His ambition was to join the family firm of solicitors, Jardine, Scott & Tan, which specialised in civil litigation and human rights law. The young lawyer, Oliver Tan, saw himself as a defender of civil rights. He passionately believed in three basic freedoms for all people-freedom of conscience, freedom of association and freedom of expression. Unfortunately, none of those freedoms was guaranteed in his homeland, Malaysia.

Oliver Tan was a true Penangite. He loved the island's superb location and natural beauty. He also knew its long colonial history, its rich heritage, its stunning colonial architecture, its bustling bazaars, its esplanade and sandy beaches. He loved the sights, sounds and smells of George Town which still retained a tangible colonial ambiance reflected in its street names – Pitt Street, King Street, Carnarvon Street, Campbell Street, etc. Most of all he loved its coffee houses and banana leaf rice restaurants famous for their kai fan,[1] bak kut teh,[2] and Penang laksa.[3] Penang was a good place to live, even though urban planning left a lot to be desired, especially the building of high-rise apartments on hill slopes. However, there was good racial and religious harmony between the Chinese, Malays and Indians. There were temples, mosques and churches all over the island and there were few instances of racial or religious strife, in contrast to many other parts of Malaysia. When his friends came from Kuala Lumpur to visit Penang, Oliver Tan took great delight in showing them the island's historical and cultural glories – Penang Museum and Art Gallery, St. George's Church and Fort Cornwallis where Sir Francis Light landed in 1786 and talked the Sultan of Kedah into signing over the island to the British. He would then take them for a scenic drive along Gurney Drive to the island's famed beaches at Batu Ferringhi, taking in a brief visit to the Botanical Gardens on the way back to high tea at the Eastern & Oriental Hotel.

When Oliver Tan returned to Penang in the summer of 2009, the political landscape had changed beyond recognition. The general election in March of that year had been a political tsunami that the ruling coalition had not quite come to terms with. The stranglehold of the ruling party had been broken and the opposition took control of the state government in Penang, Perak, Selangor, Kedah and Kelantan. However, in the land of dirty tricks, the general perception was that certain elements in BN ruling party [4] would do whatever it took to cling on to power. They would demonise and denigrate the opposition and with the co-operation of the police, have its leader sent to the Kamunting.[5] There would also be a concerted government campaign against freedom of expression and freedom of assembly. Taxi drivers in Penang would tell you that the 'little pharaohs' in Putrajaya had already adopted a multi-pronged approach, using a variety of laws to curb expression. The *Printing Presses and Publications Act* (1984) was used to intimidate newspapers critical of the government. Books critical of government policy were banned and the broadcast media were censored. A special unit was set up to control the Internet. Arrests and harassment under the Sedition Act continued. What the government gurus failed to appreciate was that the more your muzzle freedom of expression, the more it goes underground.

Penangites have always considered themselves different from other Malaysians. They are more 'opinionated' than mainlanders and it is not surprising that some of the nation's most controversial and outspoken characters have come from Penang. One such character was Dr. Samuel Mohan, an academic and educational consultant who took the Federal government to task over its proposed new Secondary school history syllabus and textbooks. He pointed out that the revised state-sponsored history textbooks contained exaggerations and mistakes. They were being used to promote the notion of a Malay Muslim cultural identity to the exclusion of other races and religions. The government had decided to extend the history syllabus by adding new elements on 'patriotism', 'citizenship' and 'the constitution'. However, in Dr. Mohan's view, these new elements were intended to enhance the political philosophy of the ruling party and to soften up students to Islam with a biased history syllabus. He pointed out, for instance, that the *One Malaysia* [6] concept was a party-political agenda and not part of the Rukun Malaysia.[7] There was, he claimed, a conscious and concerted attempt at propagandising the ruling party's position and inserting Islamic elements into the curriculum.

Dr. Mohan was asked to explain his views which he did in a paper called 'Subversion in the Classroom'. His thesis was that the teaching of history was being distorted by an ethno-nationalist approach. It had become Malay-centric and politically biased. It glossed over or de-emphasised many important phases of the nation's history, for instance, the role of the Chinese and the crucial role of Kapitan Yap Ai Loy as the founder of Kuala Lumpur; the rise and fall of the Malacca empire; the White Rajah rule in Sarawak; the 60 years of administration of Sabah by the British Chartered Company; the role of the Mission schools; the exploitation of Indian and Ceylonese workers on the plantations; the Japanese invasion and Japan's wartime support for Malay nationalist aspirations; the Malaysian Emergency and the role of Chin Peng and the MNLA; the 'Konfrontasi'[8] with Indonesia, and failure to accord Chinese, Indian and other indigenous people equal historical space. In his analysis, national history textbooks were being manipulated by the government to support a Malay Muslim hegemony and did not present objective historical truth. History textbooks had become one of the channels of subtle indoctrination. Their obsession with the concept of 'ketuanan Melayu'[9] suggested that the country belonged to the Malays and that all other people were 'bangsa asing'[10] and 'pendatang'.[11] The implication was that all non-Malays were not to be trusted and their presence in Malaysia was taking something away from the Malays. The 'little pharaohs' in the Ministry of Education viewed history only through the lens of one race and one religion. In Dr. Mohan's analysis, there was a clear correlation between autocratic regimes and revisionist history. The most powerful member of the ruling BN coalition was the United Malays National Organisation

(UMNO) [12] and its cultural marker was the fabled 'keris',[13] the symbol of race-based politics.

UMNO was not pleased with Dr. Mohan's reading of the situation. It was stated that the new history programme was merely an instrument for forging a united Malaysia. However, when letters began to appear in the press agreeing with Dr. Mohan's claim that the government was subverting the teaching of history, the government response became more personal and aggressive and it was not long before Dr. Mohan was charged with sedition. The young lawyer Oliver Tan was called upon to defend the eminent historian.

When it came to suppressing freedom of expression, Malaysia had a range of tools it could use to harass and silence its critics. It could invoke the provisions of the *Printing Presses and Publications Act, 1984* (PPPA). However, it was hardly necessary to do so, since the government maintained a monopoly on ownership of the print media. Much more sinister was the archaic *Sedition Act* (1948) which was the government's favourite instrument to threaten, arrest and charge Malaysians. The reach of the *Sedition Act* was very wide. For instance, it was a crime to question the special rights and privileges of the bumiputeras,[14] to show disrespect or even 'disaffection' against the rulers, or to voice any criticism of Islam. Cartoonists, singers, churchmen, even the Bar Council had been investigated under the *Sedition Act*. There was no longer room for dissent. Actions by the police in breaking up a number of a lawful protests suggested that Malaysia was becoming a police state. That extraordinary demonstration of abuse of power was due, in Dr. Mohan's view, to the nationalistic indoctrination of Malay youth in the classroom and the cultural worship of the kris. However, in the government's eyes, Dr. Mohan's allegation of gross bias in the teaching of history was tantamount to sedition.

The problem for the Federal government and the police was how to silence the voice of a learned academic whose views resonated with all educated young Malaysians, whether Malay, Chinese, or Indian. They could resort to dirty tricks, namely, a trumped-up charge of sexual abuse or corruption. However, the police knew that it would be futile to bring a change of sexual abuse against Dr. Mohan. That particular ploy had been overplayed in a number of recent high-profile cases. The rakyat[16] would never believe yet another sodomy story. Moreover, everyone knew that

Dr. Mohan was a God-fearing man who attended church every Sunday and raised his family in a pious Christian manner. Neither could the police link Dr. Mohan to corruption since the ruling party was plagued with corruption, not least being the mysterious 'disappearance' of Rm 12.5 billion allocated for the Port Klang Free Zone project, described as the 'mother of all scandals'.[17] It was well known that Dr. Mohan had two powerful weapons at his disposal. Firstly, he had an expert knowledge of the history of Malaysia and Southeast Asia and he could prove that Malaysia was well on its way to becoming a police state. Secondly, he was a brilliant speaker and writer, equally at home in English, Malay or Tamil. When it came to academic debate, he had few rivals. Hence, it was decided to fabricate a case of sedition against him, accusing him of disseminating false reports prejudicial to racial harmony in the country. Various government lackeys would provide compelling evidence that the new history syllabus and textbooks were not politically motivated nor biased in favour of one political group or religion.

Oliver Tan knew that the case against Dr. Mohan was trivial, spurious and fabricated but that did not matter if the judge was acting on instructions from the government. Even if the case was dismissed, the prosecution would appeal it. The Federal hounds were snarling at the gate, baying for blood. It was clear to all concerned that Dr. Mohan would get a lengthy prison sentence and possibly a heavy fine. In a police state, the accused person is presumed guilty from the outset. Eventually, Dr. Mohan got his day in court. The initial hearing was a tame affair. The charges against Dr, Mohan were preferred and various preliminary matters were dealt with. Oliver Tan had done a detailed semantic analysis of the transcript of the alleged seditious comments in Dr. Mohan's text. He pointed out that nowhere had his client made factual assertions but had hedged his comments in phrases, such as "it would appear that…", "it seems that…", "one gets the impression that…" etc. In other words, his comments were opinions, not facts and opinions by definition cannot be true or false, hence the charge of sedition was invalid. The judge seemed quite satisfied that the case against Dr. Mohan might not have much substance. However, he needed some time to take a close look at the wording of the new draft history syllabus and textbooks and also at the transcript of Dr. Mohan's alleged defamatory comments on it. He agreed that the sedition charge against the defendant was a linguistic matter. There had to be a direct and unequivocal assertion of fact. Therefore, he needed some time to examine the wording in all relevant documents and he delayed proceedings for a month.

Even though Dr. Mohan was satisfied that his defense counsel had won the opening round, he knew only too well that the prosecution would fight the case tooth and nail. He sat down with his wife to contemplate their future. They agreed that there was no way they were going to win the case. The odds were stacked against them. Dr. Mohan's future looked decidedly bleak. He was a worried man. He had three teenage children nearing the end of their Secondary schooling. Perhaps his best bet was to do a runner. Why wait for the sword of Damocles to fall? His counsel had cleverly persuaded to judge to view the matter as a semantic issue and not to read things into Dr. Mohan's comments beyond the sense of the words used. However, even if the judge was impartial and found in his favour, his future academic career in the country was doomed. He would be black-listed and his books and articles would be banned. His cousin had emigrated to New Zealand some years previously and spoke highly of the country and its people. He suggested that Dr. Mohan might secure a good position in the University of Auckland since he was a highly regarded specialist on the history of Southeast Asia. Next day, Dr. Mohan informed Oliver Tan that he was considering emigrating to New Zealand and living a normal life in a normal country. At first, Oliver Tan disagreed, saying that they had the prosecution on the run and that the judge would find in their favour. However, on reflection, he conceded that even if they won the case, the harassment would continue and it would be a pyrrhic victory if at the end of the day the victor had to pay the ultimate price.

Accordingly, Dr. Mohan put it about that the family was moving to Johor Bahru, whereas his wife and children moved to Singapore while he arranged for their passage to New Zealand. His brother-in-law agreed to buy his house in Penang and the New Zealand High Commission agreed to let Dr. Mohan and his family have a temporary residence permit with the possibility of upgrading to permanent residence if certain conditions were met. And so, Malaysia lost one of its most brilliant academics and Malaysia's loss was New Zealand's gain. In a brief note to Oliver Tan from Auckland, Dr. Mohan noted the 'the trains actually run-on time and amazingly, people queue, which for me is the acid test of civilization.' He still remembered the sheer horror of travelling on the primitive RTM trains from Central Station to Klang-a truly Third World experience. However, he remains a true Malaysian at heart and he is confident that one day the 'New Malaysia' will become an abode of peace, tolerance and representative democracy.

ENDNOTES:

1 *kai fan*: chicken rice.
2 *bak kut teh*: a herbal pork rib soup
3 *Penang laksa*: a Chinese dish consisting of rice noodles served in a hot soup
4 *BN: Barisan Nasional* (National Front)-the ruling coalition of 14 component political parties, of which UMNO, (representing the Malays), MCA (representing the Chinese) and MIC (representing the Indians) are the largest.
5 *Kamunting:* A town in Perak famous for its prison camp for detainees under the Internal Security Act. Also known as Malaysia's Gitmo.
6 *'One Malaysia'*: The political slogan and programme of BN whereby all Malaysians have the same rights, entitlements and opportunities, which was obviously not the case at the time of this story.
7 *Rukun Malaysia*: the social contract between the government and the governed (rakyat).
8 *Konfrontasi*: The Indonesia-Malaysia confrontation (1963-66) stemming from Indonesia's opposition to the creation of the Federation of Malaysia in 1963 and control of the island of Borneo.
9 *ketuanan Melayu*: Malay supremacy
10 *bangsa asing*: foreign races
11 *pendatang*: immigrants
12 *UMNO:* The largest Malay political party in the BN coalition which ruled Malaysia from Independence until May 2018.
13 *keris:* The fabled dagger of the Malay people. 'No object has the singular status, value and meaning like the keris.' (Farish A. Noor.2009. *What Your Teacher did not Tell You*. p.20)
14 *bumiputera*: A Malaysian of indigenous Malay origin; literally 'a son of the soil.'
15 *rakyat*: the common people
16 *'Mother of All Scandals'*: A book by Lim Kit Siang (2009). Petaling Jaya: Democratic Action Party.

For more on the erasing of history in Malaysia, see Chapter 1 of Farish A. Noor (2009). *'What Your Teacher Didn't Tell You'*. Matahari Books.

GOLD RUSH IN PAHANG

Pahang is the belly of West Malaysia. It is a huge state-the biggest in the country. It is also a tourist wonderland, filled with mountains, rainforest, caves and sandy beaches. What makes Pahang special, apart from its scenic beauty, is the cool air. There, in the highlands, the visitor can enjoy a respite from the stifling heat of the lowlands. In colonial times, it was the ideal place to have a hill station surrounded by a sea of greenery-rainforest and tea plantations. The most popular destinations were Cameron Highlands, Genting Highlands and Fraser's Hill. To the British colonists, those places were little pockets of 'the old country' with colonial style bungalows and chalets, rose gardens and strawberry beds in a temperate climate some 1,500 metres above sea level. At the upper end of Pahang is Taman Negara, Malaysia's oldest and largest virginal rainforest, home to an estimated 200 species of mammal and where in olden times 'noosing elephants' and hunting tigers were royal sports.

The Malay Peninsula has a long tradition of gold mining but where did the gold come from? Marco Polo made reference to a large and wealthy province called Lokak where gold abounded in the river beds. Hence, it is reasonable to speculate that Raub[1] in Pahang may have been that place-the 'golden city', the El Dorado of Malaya. It was said that gold mining in the Raub district dated back over 800 years when Mon Khemer Cambodians came to Pahang on elephants to obtain gold to adorn their majestic temples in Ankor Wat (Moore & Cubitt, 2000).

In the early days, mining was done by dulang washers[2] who panned for gold in the river beds. All of that changed in 1889 when the Raub

Australian Gold Mining Company, spearheaded by William Bibby, arrived and introduced open cast mining. Bibby discovered rich gold-bearing seams at nearby Bukit Koman in 1894 and his company sank several shafts. The deposits were similar to the one in Ballarat-deep structures with high-grade ore shoots. The whole area became a rabbit warren of tunnels, accessed by shafts reaching almost 300 metres. People in Raub could feel the vibration of the earth under their feet as drilling and blasting took place. By the turn of the century, gold mining had transformed the swampy belukar[3] of Raub into a prosperous township with a population of 3,500 people, mostly Australians and Chinese.

One of the early settlers in Raub was Felix Flynn from Ballarat. His father, Rory Flynn and two of his uncles were caught stealing sheep from Major Mahon's estate in Strokestown in County Roscommon and they were transported to Australia, which at that time was a penal colony. Fortunately for the Flynns, in the State of Victoria, convicts who could prove that they had been deported for trivial reasons, such as sheep stealing, were allowed to appeal their sentences and if reprieved, were designated as 'free men' who had the right to seek employment in the Victorian gold fields. Rory Flynn settled in Ballarat and spent the rest of his days as a 'bomber' in the mines. In 1910, his son Felix followed in his footsteps as a miner. Unfortunately, Ballarat's last mine closed down in 1918. The young Felix had no desire to remain in a town that was dying on its feet. He and many of his work mates were informed that William Bibby had struck gold in Bukit Koman, near Raub in Pahang. The miners were offered very attractive terms and conditions to join Bibby's Gold Mining Company.

Raub was already a boomtown when Felix arrived in 1920. There were shops, a bank, bars, a school, a police station and a small hydroelectric power station. As the town thrived, so did colonial life. Soon there were cricket pitches, tennis courts and swimming pools. Most of the miners were Australians and some of them purchased land on nearby Fraser's Hill and had Australian type bungalows built on it. In that scenic environment, some distance from the mines, the air was always cool and refreshing so that one could really enjoy life and experience a stress-free lifestyle. Some of the miners were Chinese and Indians but the Malays did not fancy the idea of living and working underground like a mole. The Australians ran the show. There was no racial or religious strife as everyone was making good money and enjoying the good life in a well-ordered township. Certainly, Felix found Raub very much to his liking. The food in the canteen was first class and one could relax over a beer in one of the many bars in town.

However, life in the mines was not all fun. Working underground in dimly lit tunnels was a hard and hazardous occupation. The daily drilling and blasting to extract the ore called for extreme physical fitness and mental alertness on the part of the miners. It demanded long hours of vigilance and strict adherence to safety regulations. Bibby's mine at Bukit Koman was a model of its kind. The shafts were serviced every week and the tunnels were inspected regularly. Ventilation ducts carried fresh air into the mines and reserves of fresh drinking water were supplied daily. However, there was no early warning system to tell the miners when a tremor might occur or an explosion due to methane gas. A tremor is every miner's nightmare. It can happen at any time and cause untold havoc, just like a minor earthquake. At Raub, the whole area below the town was honeycombed with tunnels and one day, due to compression and subsidence, a section of the mine wall caved in, trapping Felix and ten other miners in a chamber with no way out. The men were sent flying in all directions but fortunately there was no loss of life. The tremor lasted a mere 30 seconds. Felix was flung against the mine wall like a rag doll. A lump of quartz hit his head and he lost consciousness. He found himself tumbling down a dark tunnel on his way to eternity. At that moment, he remembered saying to himself: 'So this is how it all ends.' In his delirium, he saw his grandfather James who had worked on Major Mahon's estate in Strokestown during the Great Famine.[4] He was in a team of stone masons who were paid a penny a day to build a six-foot-high wall around the estate. Felix recalled his grandfather's graphic account of the Great Famine in Roscommon when the potato crop failed due to blight and people starved in a land of plenty. However, the plenty was in the hands of greedy landlords who chose to export their corn and beef rather than feed the starving multitude. James Flynn had witnessed corpses lying unburied in the streets for days, sometimes gnawed by dogs and rats. Destitute Catholics in Roscommon had three choices. They could die of hunger, or beg for food in Protestant-run soup kitchens, or catch the 'coffin ship' to Canada.

Felix's father, Rory was a young man of 18 years when he and his two brothers were charged with and convicted of stealing sheep from Major Mahon's estate. They were transported to Australia in 1848, along with 240 other felons. Felix was given a full account of the barbaric treatment meted out to the deportees on their way to the penal servitude.

Somehow, the Flynns always seemed to be in the wrong place at the wrong time. Felix's uncle Ned was shot for his part in the unrest at the Eureka Stockade.[5] The leaders of the rebellion were Irish and twenty-two of them were shot in cold blood by the security forces. His other uncle Frank had enlisted in the army and was gunned down at Gallipoli [6] in 1916 during a frontal assault on the enemy. Felix remembered being told that his uncle Frank had been 'shot in the Dardanelles', which in his ignorance of geography, he understood to be the abdomen.

Now, it seemed, Felix was about to add one more chapter to the blood and tears saga of the Flynn clan. Posterity would learn that he was done to death by a tremor in a gold mine some 300 metres below the town of Raub in Pahang. However, when he opened his eyes, he found himself staring into the headlamp on Pete Murray's helmet and when he heard him call out: 'He's ok, mates', he knew that he was still in the land of the living. He was badly shaken, in great pain, and there was a swelling the size of a cricket ball on his left temple. He was so weak he could hardly move. He was told that a rescue team had already been assembled and lowered into the shaft. Its mission was to clear a path through the caved-in section of the mine and get the miners out as quickly as possible. The men worked hard to clear the slag but progress was slow and it was impossible to say how long it would take to reach the trapped miners. There was little Felix could do except sit and wait. His work mates began clearing away the slag on their side and made a passage wide enough for a person to get through. It was hard work for men badly shaken by the tremor and weakened by lack of food. At last, a chink of light appeared in the tunnel and Pete Murray exclaimed: 'Mafeking relieved!'[7] Felix could barely move and his comrades strapped him to an old rope ladder and crouching low, carried him like a wounded soldier.

It was a moment of great joy and relief for all concerned. William Bibby greeted the miners at the mine head and they were treated like war heroes when they finally emerged from the shaft cage. An old sepia photograph shows them looking like an exhausted party of men on one of

Scott's expeditions across polar ice-cap returning to base camp. One could see the hardship etched on their faces. By that time, Felix had recovered somewhat from his ordeal. Perhaps the bad karma that had dogged the Flynn clan for centuries was finally broken.

Felix remained in Rauf until 1941 when Japanese troops invaded Malaya and all mining operations in Bukit Koman came to a grinding halt. Then, he returned home to Ballarat, with fond memories of his 20 years in Pahang. We do not know much about his private life as he was a thoroughly private person. We do know, however, that while in Raub, he married a Chinese woman and they had a large family, who later achieved great academic success at the University of Ballarat. When asked why his children looked oriental, Felix replied: 'Sure, aren't they Chinese Irish?'

ENDNOTES:

1   *Raub*: A town in Pahang, once famous as a gold-mining town.
2   *dulang washing*: The process by which gold is separated from gravel and mud by agitation and washing. In Malay, the word 'dulang' means pan.
3   *belukar*: The Malay for bush or wild land.
4   *The Great Famine*: Ireland's greatest disaster between 1845 and 1850, when blight devastated the potato crop and two million Irish people died or emigrated. See Campbell, S. J. (1994). *The Great Irish Famine*. Famine Museum, Strokestown.
5   *Eureka Stockade*: The Eureka rebellion led by Peter Lalor in 1854. A short-lived revolt against petty officialdom by hundreds of gold miners. It was seen as the dawn of democracy in Australia.
6   *Gallipoli*: In World War 1, scene of the bloody campaign which took place on the Gallipoli peninsula on the European side of the Dardanelles in 1915-16.
7   *Mafeking relieved:* The lifting of the siege of Mafeking during the Second Boer War in South Africa 1899-1900.

14
MAN ON A MISSION

Hadi Razal dropped out of high school in Form 2. Hell, what was the use of education in the Kuala Lumpur jungle? He knew that had he stayed on at school he would have become a serial killer. He would have taken out quite a few of the teachers in the school, especially all the faggots and 'holy Marys'. They had fucked him up good and proper. Those sanctimonious morons, full of pomposity, attitude and moral rectitude had clashed with him once too often. For instance, Miss Timms, his science teacher, had called him a degenerate. She needed a good bashing and one day he might do a job on her. In one lesson, the topic was the identification of flowers by their colour, shape and scent. Each group was given a specimen flower to examine. Hadi's group was given a sprig of hibiscus, which grew profusely in the hedges around the school. It was the pink variety. So, what colour was it? The group chorused: 'Pink, miss.'

'How silly!' spat Miss Timms. 'Open your books on page 49. Look at the list of common flowering plants and their characteristics. What colour is in the book? Red, of course.' Hadi gave up. When the teacher is as thick as a double ditch, there's no point arguing. She wanted the students to say that a pink flower was red. She was teaching them how to lie. Silly cow. On another occasion, she was teaching the classification of mammals into vertebrates and non-vertebrates. She pointed to various animals in a chart and asked the class to say whether they were vertebrates or non-vertebrates. She pointed to a fish and the class chorused: 'Vertebrate, Miss.' She said: 'Now, let's see' and she produced a large plastic fish, bent it double and demonstrated quite clearly that fishes were non-vertebrates. Hadi wondered how she could possibly have failed to notice the large backbone in the fish on her dinner plate. But that was education Malaysian style. All the lessons were of the 'chalk and talk', boring and banal.

Hadi had no problem with being a Muslim but the religious teacher, Farouk, was a real freak. He and Hadi had many an unpleasant contretemps over dress code, swearing, smoking and religious obligations. Farouk didn't understand the Qur'an just as so-called Christians didn't understand the Bible. They were all moralistic morons. The only teacher he really liked was Miss Gibson, his English teacher. She was great fun and her lessons were always bubbly.

Outside the school, things were much worse. Kuala Lumpur (KL) was a magnet for the lowest life forms in Malaysia. There, you did not meet the charming and honest Malays of Kedah and the other states. Instead, you came across urban bandits, bent politicians, government officials with greasy palms, pimps who ran vice dens. The streets were awash with cannabis, heroin and syabu. Common decency and honesty were scarce commodities in the streets of KL. People littered the streets, spat in public, smoked in non-smoking areas and behaved like a rugby scrum when boarding a bus or train. Pickpockets lurked round every corner and corruption hung in the air like the haze that blew in from Sumatra. Everyone was out to do you and you had to be street wise. How could it be otherwise? Politicians were corrupt to the core-a shower of plutocrats-government by the wealthy for the wealthy. A one-party state. Fuck the Chinese and Indians and God help the non-Malays in Sabah and Sarawak. Hadi regarded himself as a good Muslim, but the religious freaks were becoming more intolerant and fundamentalist by the week, banning everything that was normal and human, like sex, personal freedom, alcohol, religious freedom, modern music, even yoga. Malaysia was becoming a Taliban state. Any show of protest or democracy was suppressed and the pigs hit you with the Internal Security Act (ISA).[1] Just like in China, Burma and Iran, a brotherhood of bandits was running the show. Not surprisingly, those marginalized and beaten turned to crime and every part of the city and the Klang Valley had its quota of gangsters. One did not become a gangster in KL; the system bred gangsters just as its clammy climate bred mosquitoes, cockroaches and other vermin. Hadi and his mates had formed a gang called The Rotts. Totally non-sectarian, non-racial and non-sexist. Their agenda was to keep their patch decent, free of perverts and law-abiding. There were a lot of things that needed sorting out in his home area, Kepong.

Hadi did not look like a gangster; more like a Korean pop singer. Tall, slim, with an Adonis body. Long black hair sleeked back and tied in a ponytail. Clean shaven with a baby face. The sort of handsome hulk that gave girls a wet dream. The only hint of gangsterism was his cold grey eyes-the eyes of a killer. He was a mean fighter. Never carried a gun, only a flick-knife. Knew every trick in the book. A Kung Fu king. He was no fool. Had had read every page of Sun Tzu's (2010) *The Art of War*.[2] That was his bible. The grand master spoke the truth. 'Know your enemy and do not trust your friends. In the jungle, you don't know who your friends are.' Prophetic words.

Hadi saw himself as a perfectly ordinary person, with a moral mission. He didn't do drugs. He didn't chase skirt. He didn't rob the widow. Man, he was biblical. Not religious. Just biblical. A just man. Unlike the toffee-nosed government mandarins swanning around in their state cars, up to their necks in crime, only they never called it such. They called it government business. When you have the power, you can make your own definitions. A bunch of morons who in Hadi's words were as crooked as a dog's hind leg. He had a way with words. On one occasion, referring to a certain not-too-bright government minister, he said: 'All his grey matter is in his back passage.'

One of the things that really offended Hadi was the 'Open Mouth Gawk'. Whenever he walked down the street, minding his own business, people would stop and stare at him. One day a middle-age lady really got to him. She seemed to think that Hadi had arrived from outer space and she stood there, her mouth wide open, as much as to say: 'Arrest that man. He must be an alien.' Obviously, a brain-washed UMNO [3] supporter. Hadi did not ever want to hit a woman but he made an exception on that occasion. He kneed her in the groin and stuffed his ice-cream into her open mouth. Nothing like ice-cream for shutting gobs. He was a man on a mission. He would teach people in Kepong and KL the one thing they lacked most-manners. His area was plagued with crime-drugs, mugging, rape, child abuse, sex trafficking, house breaking and more. He formed The Rotts to keep his patch clean and law-abiding. Concerned citizens turned to Hadi and his mates for protection. They did not trust the police-greedy, money-grabbing bastards. They were in cahoots with the drug traffickers, on a commission basis. Hadi knew the scene all too well.

The Rotts were not the only show in town. Most of the gangs were Chinese and you did not mess with the Triads. They lopped off your hands or your balls. But they respected territorial integrity. One had to avoid gang warfare at any cost. Chinese Triads were part and parcel of KL culture but there was no way The Rotts would ever allow new-comers-Iranians, Nigerians, and Indonesians to make a fortune selling dope to kids on the streets of Kepong and KL. The Rotts worked in cooperation with like-minded gangs in Rawang, Seremban, Brickfields and the Klang Valley. A brotherhood of law enforcers.

Contrary to stories in the press and the blood-and-gore shown in movies, not all gangs were thugs, junkies and juvenile delinquents. Sure, The Rotts took stuff from stores and supermarkets, but they drew the line at sexual molestation, mugging and bag-snatching. In every organization, there is bound to be the occasional internal feuding. Movies tend to focus on gang warfare and give gangsters a bad name. The Rotts operated a strict code based on respect and good manners. Their mission was entirely moral and social. They beat up the jerks that harassed young females. They collared pick pockets and gave them such a bashing that they squealed like stuck pigs. The traffic cops might turn a blind eye to rich people parking their BMWs all over the place but Hadi and his gang soon sorted them. They sprayed the windows with black enamel. One had to teach the punks good manners.

Hadi's second-in-command was an Indian chap, Vince Kumar-a hard nut from Klang. Took no guff from anyone. Moreover, unlike the dudes in other gangs, he was intelligent. Sadly, one day he was done for shop lifting. The pigs beat him up, not because of the item he had lifted but because he was Indian and they hated anyone from Klang. Vince knew all the bad Malay jokes about Indians, for instance, if you came across a snake and an Indian at the same time, what would you do? Answer: Kill the Indian first. Vince was held in police detention for a week and beaten every day because he would not rat on Hadi and the gang. Then they threw him out of a 4th floor window of the Remand Home. There was no inquest. The police report stated that 'the inmate, a member of a well-known Kepong gang, had tried to escape by jumping from the window…' The swine. But there would be retribution. Oh yes, Hadi would see to that personally.

Some weeks later, Hadi discovered a convoy of water cannon parked along a side street off Jalan Imbi in readiness for a protest march that weekend. The riot police were going to smash the protesters as usual, label them subversives and grab the leaders under the ISA. Hadi managed to hijack one of the tankers under cover of dark, had it emptied of water and re-filled with raw sewage. Then he drove to Kepong police station and sprayed it with the brown stuff. Just a token payback for the murder of Vince. Naturally, he lay low for a week knowing that every cop in KL was out to nab him. Eventually, they pinned it on a rival gang and had them sent to the salt mines. Allah be praised. Sun Tzu would have been impressed; killing two birds with one stone.

It is a popular myth that KL gangs beat up girls. The Rotts did not tolerate any sexual harassment of girls. Even if the pussy cats were over-exposed and showed a bit of leg, that was their entitlement. Gays were not allowed to join the club, not that they tried to but a person's sexual orientation was their own affair and there would be no beating up of gays, lesbians or Mak Nyah.[4] Not so, perverts and child molesters. They had crossed the line and would be sent to Dr. Fong. That was the nickname of Roy Fong who worked in an abattoir in Port Klang and knew a thing or two about neutering. He loved doing a job on perverts with his rusty knife.

It was not long before Kepong was the safest, most crime-free town in Selangor. Time to hit the golden triangle-central KL. Lots of loose cannon in the area-mostly shitheads and pimps from Indonesia, Iran, Nigeria and other Third World ghettos. Up to every form of villainy known to man. KL was becoming the crime capital of Southeast Asia. Even the government admitted that crime had risen by 85% in recent years. Each year, over 300 sexual assault cases went to court but only 4% resulted in a conviction. Hundreds more remained unreported. Indonesian maids were treated like sex slaves. The victims complained but nothing was done because it was well known that Malay men liked a bit on the side. Hadi knew that he and his gang could not stem the flow of ordinary crime in KL. All they could do was to take out gross offenders-serial killers who preyed violently on women, child abusers, drug traffickers and defilers of places of worship. The main weapon was not the gun or the parang, but information. Hadi could not understand why the police had it in for him and his boys. After all, they were on the same side, the only difference being that The Rotts got results. The police were too busy chasing after subversives. In many areas, for instance Klang, Subang, Brickfields and Seremban you did not go out after dark. You might be mugged. Correction. You would be mugged. What did the wise men in the government do? Nothing. Oh yes, there was a lot of talk of ridding the capital of criminal elements; there would be zero tolerance of crime but they themselves were in it up to their necks. Still, it made good copy to get expert criminologists to give workshops explaining the socio-economic and cultural sources of crime. What a load of old bull! Psychos blamed it all on television. Kids were immersed in US street crime, Bollywood blood and gore movies and Chinese chop-and-kill movies. Hence, the wise ones concluded that kids could not distinguish between gangster movies and real life. Of course, they could. What a cop out! The church pleaded for tolerance and understanding. We must hate crime but love the criminal. What horse manure! Nobody wanted to face the cold truth. Criminals were evil bastards. Criminality, like addiction, was genetic. Criminals were born, not made. End of story. They had to be eliminated like vermin.

The Rotts always had plenty of money, which in Hadi's words was 'borrowed from society'. The gang's paymaster was Pitbull, a smart Chinese hulk with the personality of a. For him, getting money out of an ATM machine was like taking candy from a kid. You just looked over the person's shoulder and noted the six-digit password. Taking money from the rich and powerful was not, in Hadi's view, dishonourable. Somebody had to pay the piper and most people had so much spare cash they never missed the odd thousand. The Rotts would never take from the poor. They'd target only the rich in their posh outfits, Rolex watches and Prada bags. The scum of the earth. Mostly members of the political mafia. Not only Malays but also Chinese and Indian cling-ons. On one raid, Pitbull acquired a large safe full of banknotes from the offices of an insurance company. It took him all of 30 seconds to figure out the combination.

Pitbull was also into cybercrime. He knew how to hack into banking websites and rip off usernames, passwords and credit card details. However, he was quite selective in choosing his targets. He targeted only very rich people with 'Datuk' before their name since, in his mind, they were bandits who had siphoned off public funds. Corrupt bastards. Hence, it was no crime to steal from robbers. They dare not report the crime since the last thing they wanted was a police investigation into their transactions. Beyond 'ordinary' crime, there was the much more sinister world of white-collar crime carried out by the great and good. It included corrupt deals by bent politicians, bent police officers, bent judges and bent contractors. They were brothers in crime-the golden circle. The classic case of high-level crime was the RM 12.5 billion Port Klang Free Zone rip-off.[5] That's a lot of dosh that went into deep pockets. One writer referred to it as the 'mother of all scandals' and the then PM called it 'a crime without criminals'. Lovely words. But were the criminals brought to justice and the stolen money refunded? Come on, this is Malaysia. Such matters are best brushed under the carpet. A fish rots from the head down and that is basically the problem in KL. Criminality percolates down from the top echelon of government, through layers of cling-ons. All members of the mafia get a slice of the salami. Then, there's no money left for the rakyat.[6] Well, damn the rakyat! Let them eat grass. Some said that Hadi was full of bile and counter culture. A rebel without a cause. However, he was no anarchist. All he wanted was a just society. He disliked the PM in particular since he was up to his neck in corruption scandals. Sadly, the concepts of accountability and transparency were unknown in government circles. According to Hadi, the ruling BN coalition was a self-serving mafia.

In crime movies, there is always a nemesis. The anti-hero gets cooked in the end. The Ned Kellys of this world cannot be allowed to win. And so, it was with Hadi Razal. It all began in Kepong when several teenage girls were raped. Hadi conferred with his new second-in-command, the fearsome Pitbull, who lived in Bukit Nanas. An old boy of St. George's. A real stinker. His real name was Dennis Chin. He was as strong as an ox, with broad shoulders and a neck like an anaconda. You did not mess with Pitbull, the meanest drifter in Bukit Nanas. He scored straight As in his Cambridge A-level examinations. He should have been awarded a scholarship to study abroad but there was no way the government was going to fund a Chinese Christian for four years at a British university. The Selangor grants committee claimed that only Bumiputeras[7] had the right to receive government support, even though the Constitution said otherwise.

And so, he became a drifter. Used to help out in his dad's motorbike repair workshop. Got involved in motorbike racing. Loved the sport.

Pitbull had the nose of a sniffer dog. It was he who tracked down the rapist. A lone Pakistani wanker. Well, either Pitbull or Hadi would have to teach him some manners. Hadi decided it was his call. His long-standing girlfriend agreed to act as a decoy. Her name was Linda Loo and in KL folklore she was regarded as an urban Pontianak.[8] Spiky haired, tattooed arms, metal studs implanted in an otherwise pretty face. A real goer. Her default dress code was a tank top and skin-tight jeans. On this occasion, she dressed down. Hot pants and lots of glam. They made a good team, Linda and Hadi. He was Malay Muslim and she was Chinese Christian. A deadly combination.

She called the Pakistani taxi driver. Told him to take her to the University of Malaya. No problem. He'd give her a discount on account of her being a student. They set off. What the driver did not know was that Hadi was tailing them on his motorbike. Linda pretended to call someone on campus every now and then. 'On the road, sweet pea. See you soon.' There was roadworks on the Federal Highway near the university and they had to take a detour into Section 12. It was getting dark and the driver went: 'Did you hear that?' The engine began chugging.

'What's up?' asked Linda. 'Is there a rattle in the engine?'

'Not to worry. I know how to fix it. Only takes a minute or two'.

He stopped the car, got out and began checking under the bonnet. He asked Linda to hold the flash light. Then he grabbed her, rolled her down a grassy slope and began to undo his trousers. But Hadi was onto him in a flash. He caught the rapist red handed, out of trousers. There was no confrontation, no final words, just a quick kill. He slit the throat from ear to ear and kicked the dying body down the embankment. Then he and Linda returned to Kepong, stopping at Pappa Rich for a coffee. A job well done. No fuss. No complications. And more importantly, a killing without a trace. No tell-tale DNA. The perfect job. They were joined by Pitbull and they shared the good news with him.

However, some weeks later, a feud erupted between Hadi and Pitbull. Without telling his boss, Pitbull got involved in a protection racket in Kepong. Hadi was furious and ordered him to cease operations at once. Such activity was against the code. But Pitbull refused to comply. And so, a bust-up was inevitable. Pitbull was expelled from the noble company of The Rotts. Well, smart ass Hadi had something else coming. Nobody messed with Pitbull. He went to the police and snitched on his former gang leader. Sold him down the Swanee, hook line and sinker. Gave them details of the recent killing of the taxi driver. And that was the end of Hadi. He was arrested, charged with the unlawful killing of a Pakistani national. The judge allowed clemency in view of the moral dimension but still sentenced him to 10 years in prison.

However, Hadi did not remain in prison very long. As the great master Sun Tzu stated, 'In the midst of chaos, there is also opportunity.' You create chaos when the enemy least expects it. Nobody in KL expected a thunderstorm during the fasting month of Ramadan and certainly not during iftar,[9] when honest Muslims break the fast and enjoy the special dishes prepared for the daily feast. Yes, the great master also said: 'Let your plans be dark and impenetrable as night.' Pitbull may have done the dirt on Hadi but his comrades in Kepong did not desert him. One evening during iftar, a thunderstorm hit Kepong Prison. Some 20 hooded gang members on motorcycles fire bombed the prison setting fire to the west wing where Hadi was ready and waiting to make his exit. In the ensuing confusion, the security staff were caught off guard and the prison gates were opened to allow the fire engines in. Hadi and the gang made off in a cloud of smoke as giant flames rent the night sky over the prison.

Nobody knows what happened to Hadi subsequently. He simply disappeared but is believed to be alive and well somewhere in the Klang Valley. However, very soon after his departure, ill-mannered people re-appeared in the streets of Kepong and KL and pickpockets, drug dealers and sex offenders were back in business.

ENDNOTES:

1   *ISA*: Internal Security Act. (1960). This notorious piece of legislation was introduced by the British to quell acts of terrorism and subversion after the Emergency. It was framed by the British lawyer and writer Hugh Hickling

in 1960. It was frequently used by the government to intimidate political opponents.

2 *Sun Tzu*: (545-470 BC). An ancient Chinese military strategist and philosopher.

3 *UMNO*: The anchor party in the BN coalition that ruled Malaysia from Independence to 2018.

4 *Mak Nyah*: The transsexual community in Malaysia.

5 *Port Klang Free Zone*: See *Mother of All Scandals* by Lim Kit Siang (2009). Petaling Jaya.

6 *rakyat:* the common people

7 *bumiputera*: A Malaysian of indigenous Malay origin; literally 'a son of the soil.'

8 *Pontianak*: The dreaded vampire of Indonesian folklore, said to appear young and beautiful in order to attract male victims.

9 *iftar*: The meal with which Muslims end their daily Ramadan fast at sunset.

15

TROUBLE IN PARADISE

He who marries a beautiful woman marries
trouble. [An old Malay saying]

Tommy Carmody was as Dublin as could be, a true son of the city, born
and bred in the Liberties[1] and educated by the Christian Brothers in Synge
Street. He was a bright lad and went on to earn a BA degree in Language
and Linguistics at Trinity College. At that time in the early 80s, the Irish
economy was in poor shape and jobs were as scarce as hens' teeth. So,
he went to London where he worked part-time in an English Language
Centre for two years after which he enrolled on the MA program in
Applied Linguistics at the University of Essex. On graduation he returned
to Dublin, but he still could not find work. Then in July 1986 he accepted
a job offer in the Language Centre of the University of Malaysia in Kuala
Lumpur.

Tommy left Dublin with a heavy heart. He loved the Liberties where
generations of Carmodys had been born and raised. The people there were
clannish and greeted you with a smile. It was 'old Dublin' with cobbled
streets and artisan dwellings. Not at all posh like the townlands on the
south side. Tommy was working class – the lowest of five distinct social
classes in Dublin, which was then the most class-conscious city in Europe.
He spoke the local dialect, locally known as Dublinese-the language of
Sean O'Casey's plays. However, he could easily code switch to Standard
English when in the classroom or in polite society. He told his parents that
he was bi-dialectal and they said that was fine as long as he wasn't bi-sexual!

On that score, they need not have worried. He had fancied quite a few of the well-heeled girls at TCD. However, Dublin girls will not marry an unemployed man no matter how charming he may be, and of course, it does not help when they discover that the man in question comes from the Liberties, a working-class area attuned to grim poverty and deprivation. The people there were known as 'gurriers'.[2] Why would a respectable Dublin girl be associated with a man from the ghetto?

Tommy did not pay much attention to Dublin snobbery. He lived in a world a world of his own, a world of books. He had read most of the great classics. He loved the Brontes and Jane Austen but he disliked Dickens who, in his view, was boring and banal with too many characters, too many long sentences and very little animation, no bearing of the soul. He was especially drawn to the oriental novel. He had read all Conrad's oriental novels as well as Anthony Burgess and Somerset Maugham's short stories about colonial Malaya. It was heady romantic stuff, full of colour, magic and mystery. It was a world that appealed to Tommy's imagination and he decided that it was the perfect place for a person of his particular sensibilities.

Tommy had fallen in love with all things oriental long before he set foot in Malaysia in 1986. For him it was Paradise and he loved it from day one. The countryside was like the Garden of Eden even though the cities were ghastly-modern high rise office blocks and low-cost housing estates beside a muddy stinking river. Most of the old colonial buildings had been flattened and replaced with horrid shopping centres, offices and luxury hotels. Tommy had no idea why the Kuala Lumpur (KL) city fathers wanted the tallest tower block in the world and more six-lane highways than New York City. Why didn't somebody tell them that big is not beautiful and that a concrete jungle is not a pretty sight. But they were not concerned with preserving the rich colonial heritage of the British Empire. They were interested only in making money. And that meant obliterating the past and creating an ultra-modern city with hideous buildings just like Dubai and Bangkok, with none of the grace and elegance of Singapore. However, many parts of the country had escaped the vandalism of KL, especially the northern states-Kedah, Perlis and Terengganu. There, you could find the soul of Malaysia and lovely people unpolluted by the modernism of KL and Putrajaya.

In Malaysia, one turned a blind eye to endemic corruption and the racial and religious paranoia of the ruling party that paid lip service to the concept of 'One Malaysia'. The ruling BN coalition, was not going to share the cake with the Chinese and Indians, much less the original forest people. Tommy knew, of course, that many former British colonies were run by a self-serving mafia and you do not mess with the mafia! Every expatriate working in the former British Empire knew the score. Apart from the overt racism and widespread corruption, KL was not an unpleasant place to live and work as long as you behaved like the three wise monkeys.

Tommy rented a modern high-rise apartment in Subang Jaya, a delightful well-planned suburb which was pollution free and crime free. His neighbour, Jacob Chan, was the local dentist. He and his wife Mandy often invited Tommy for a Chinese meal, usually a lavish affair that spoke volumes of Chinese culinary culture. Jacob knew the city and its many races like the back of his hand. He spoke Cantonese, Malay and English with equal fluency and he often uttered the odd phrase in French or German. He told Tommy to steer clear of religious and political discourse-very sensitive topics in a country ruled by a powerful Islamic regime. He assured Tommy that in KL 'everything is forbidden, but freely available.' That comment made a lot of sense to Tommy, a man of liberal values. In KL, bars and brothels co-exist beside mosques and churches. That is how it should be in a liberal democracy. People should be free to be saints or sinners. Malaysia had no desire to become a theocratic state like Saudi Arabia or Iran.

In the common room at the university, Tommy was a popular member. He was a gifted conversationalist and he could tell yarns until the cows came home. He had great stories about his trips into the interior of Borneo, tribal customs, rainforest lore and tales of 'hantu' [3] and the dreaded Pontianak[4], all of which were tall tales, some quite spicy. He loved travelling into the most remote parts of Sabah and Sarawak and he was astounded to discover that many of his colleagues had never been beyond the borders of Selangor. He got on especially well with lecturers from Penang, who were outspoken critics of the government. The others, for the most part, would say things like 'Of course, we all hate UMNO,[5] but we always vote for them.' 'Why?' Tommy would ask and the answer was 'because that way we all get a slice of the salami.' That statement summed up the political culture of Malaysia. The ruling party dished out the salami before the general election and won the votes of people who despised them. It was also claimed by the opposition that the dead arose and voted for the ruling party.

In Malaysia the 'undead' are very much alive in the form of 'hantu'. There, the two worlds mingle, the real and unreal and it is hard to tell the difference between them. In Ireland the fairies live only in folklore but in Malaysia and Indonesia the 'hantu' are as real as cannon balls.

Tommy was quite handsome, with fair hair and blue eyes. He was the sort of man that Malaysian women rave about, what Malay girls called 'the real stuff'. Everywhere he went, he received unexpected female adulation. Moreover, he was equally dazzled by the exotic beauty of oriental women. They were like beautiful flowers from many different regions, all exotic-sultry Malays, slim Chinese, alluring Indians as well as foreign girls from Indonesia, the Philippines, Burma, Vietnam and Cambodia. Tommy wondered how he was going to cope with such an array of natural beauty. He was surrounded by the most beautiful women on the planet. At the same time, one had to know the rules. There were strict rules of engagement in all matters pertaining to the opposite sex. Any 'close proximity' to a Muslim woman could land you in the Sharia Court. One had to be extremely vigilant, circumspect and covert. Tommy had no interest in the brazen go-go girls in the bars and nightclubs of KL. He wanted the real thing-a real romance with an oriental goddess. His friends in the university cautioned him to tread carefully because as they put it, 'you may get more than what you wish for'! However, Tommy was in no mood to heed Confucian wisdom. Rather he preferred the advice of the poet Herrick: 'Gather ye rosebuds while ye may.'

One weekend, Tommy was with friends, enjoying a pint of beer in Lanigan's Irish Pub in Jalan Sultan. The bar was crowded as usual on a Saturday evening, all the usual clientele – disaffected expatriates, assorted tourists, gays and lady-boys and various young ladies showing a bit of leg. It was time to let down one's hair and have a bit of fun. Tommy was in his element. He loved a bit of 'craic' [6] and madness. A little later, a group of young ladies made a noisy entrance and were obviously in a celebratory mood. It was a birthday bash and the girls clustered round a bottle of Grey Goose, courtesy of the bar. It was then that Tommy's eyes alighted on one of the group-a lovely dark-haired goddess, in a slinky black dress and a body of polished ebony. 'Knock me down!' uttered Tommy, unable to conceal his instant awe and arousal at the beatific vision. 'Am I dreaming or what?' His mates failed to understand Tommy's infatuation with the goddess. KL was full of such good-looking girls, many of them 'good time' girls on the make. For them, there was nothing special about the young lady in a black dress that looked as if it had been put on by a spray gun. She was just another Chindian.[7] For Tommy, however, she was the ultimate oriental beauty queen and he wanted to grab her and run away with her to Elysian fields where they would make passionate love among beds of crocuses and wild lilies. However, even in KL one cannot do such crazy things so he kept glancing in her direction, until she smiled and gave a little wave of recognition. That was all that he needed and thus began one of the great KL love stories. I shall not dwell on it here. Suffice it to say that the young lady was Amanda Chong and that she had long hoped to meet and marry an expatriate man. Could it be that at long last she had met the man of her dreams?

Within months of his arrival in KL, Tommy was a married man. He and Amanda fell in love at first sight and in due course they got married at St. Ann's Church in Port Klang. Amanda was a nominal Catholic, educated by the nuns in Port Klang. Her father, Bobby Chong, was Chinese and her mother Katya Patel was an Indian whose parents had come to Selangor to work in the tin mines in the Kinta valley in the early 20s. Mr. and Mrs. Chong ran a small restaurant which served delightful Chinese and Indian dishes. The wedding was a lavish affair, attended by over a hundred guests, including Tommy's parents and sister.

At that time, Tommy and Amanda were living in a rented apartment in Subang Jaya on the KTM railway line between KL and Port Klang. There they enjoyed wedded bliss, in a township that had everything – mega malls, restaurants, beauty salons and rows of traditional shop houses. The following year, Amanda gave birth to a beautiful baby girl, whom they christened Leanne. Tommy was earning good money at the university and he also got involved in writing and publishing English language textbooks for Secondary level students. The money was rolling in and Amanda begged Tommy to move to Bangsar, an upmarket township close to KL. Tommy was happy to do so since it was near his university. They found an old colonial bungalow there and having obtained a substantial bank loan from Maybank, they were able to purchase it. It was in poor condition but that did not matter. They renovated it and furnished it in the traditional manner with cane and teak. In matters of internal design and decor, Amanda had impeccable taste. She quickly transformed the dilapidated bungalow into a beautiful stone-clad residence. In a matter of two years, their home was valued at over a million ringgit. Everything was rosy in the garden or so it seemed. Tommy told his parents that he had a fantastic marriage-a marriage made in heaven. And he had the most adorable child in KL. However, by the end of their third year, chinks began to appear in the marriage made in heaven. The unmaking of that happy marriage is best told by Tommy. What follows is his version of events in his own words, more or less.

'Well, I'm glad it's all over. Today, I am a happily divorced man. Sadly, our happy marriage collapsed like a house of cards. I can say in all honesty that it had little to do with me. I simply married the wrong woman, a woman with an enormous ego and an insatiable lust for power and money. I was a mere stepping stone in Amanda's grand plan to join the ranks of the ultra-rich. She would obviously marry again and divorce again in order to achieve her goal. For her, divorce was like winning the lotto. There are worse things in life than dying and that's living with a smart-ass woman. I should know. I lived with a gold-digger for five long years, two years of bliss and three years of torture. It was quite frankly worse that a life sentence in Kajang Prison, the grimmest prison in Southeast Asia. It took me ages to discover that my goddess was a snake in the grass. She soon grew tired of being a housewife and she decided to return to school, taking a course in Beauty Therapy and Aromatherapy leading to the CIDESCO diploma. I gladly went along with her plan, thinking it gave her a sense of commitment and fulfillment. A woman should not be tied to the kitchen sink. She seemed to enjoy the course and having at last obtained her diploma she decided not to work in a beauty salon, which paid peanuts but to offer her services freelance to hotel clients. She had her own website and did her business online. At first, there were few callers but as time went by she was inundated with calls for body massage and other like services by clients all over KL. My good wife was happy and run off her feet. She'd go out most evening and not return until the small hours.

Incredibly, I still did not get it. Amanda would sleep during the morning and let our amah do all the cooking and cleaning. Her only interest was her diary of appointments.

Then, out of the blue, one evening my colleague Abdul Rahman phoned me inviting me for a drink at the Chariot Inn. He said he wished to discuss a certain matter with me. I was alarmed. Abdul Rahman was not the kind of man who engaged in idle gossip. He obviously had something on his mind. I dashed to the Chariot Inn and found Abdul Rahman already at the bar. 'Here' he said, handing me a large whiskey 'you'll need this.' He grimaced and putting his hand on my shoulder said: 'I'm sorry to have to tell you that your good wife is a common whore. I happen to know the janitor at the Royal Hotel and he told me that Amanda is offering her clients a good time for RM 500-a massage with a happy ending, if you see what I mean. She is obviously very good at her trade; she often sees two or three clients each evening.'

I could not believe my ears. I suspected that my wife was up to something but I had no idea that her business was pleasuring city gents. I was not prepared for such shocking news. It was like being hit over the head with a hammer. I began chain smoking and ordered another round. My mind was full of scorpions. No man will tolerate a devious cheating wife. In such a situation, most men will resort to violence and experience a burning desire to strangle the bitch. Your mood changes from disbelief, to disgust, to anger to revenge. I just wanted to get my hands on a sharp parang and sever that scheming head from that seductive body. Abdul Rahman read my mind. He kept saying: 'It's not the end of the world old boy! Don't let it develop into open warfare. Get a good divorce lawyer. It is all over with Amanda but there are plenty more fish in the sea. Sadly, you caught a crab. Take care you are not snared by the dreaded Pontianak, la!'

Poor Abdul Rahman did his best cheer me up but neither he nor anyone else could banish my gloom. There was darkness in my soul. My life was in ruins. The little vixen had sold me down the Swanee. Now you know why I say there are worse things than dying. My good friend Abdul Rahman was quite philosophical about it all. 'It's the will of Allah,' he said 'pull yourself together. Drink up, man. Keep your feet on the ground. Salvage what you can and make sure you win custody of your little girl. She will be your consolation.'

I knew that Abdul Rahman was right. My marriage was on the rocks.
There was no way out. Amanda had already filed for divorce and so it was
that we ended up in the Circuit Family Court in KL before Judge Abdul
Gani Al-Attas. It was not a pleasant experience. My wife was the Applicant
seeking divorce and favourable terms and I was the Respondent, seeking
damage limitation. My super solicitor, Ms Ratnam, had compiled a full
brief, listing my wife's many transgressions with names and dates and bank
statements. She was able to show that Amanda was earning as much as RM
1,000 each evening. My Counsel, Mr. William Tan SC cross-examined
Amanda, making it abundantly clear, in the nicest possible way, that she
had contravened every clause of our marriage contract, not to mention the
moral code of the State. He then proceeded to argue most cogently that
his client (me) was totally blameless. Hence, he pleaded that the cheating
partner should not be rewarded for her villainy but sentenced to a long
period in prison in full accordance with the provisions of The Family
Law (Divorce) Act 1994. However, that was not how the judge saw it. He
seemed to side with Amanda's Counsel, the wily Mr. Raj Kumar, who
conceded that Amanda had acted rashly but he also proposed that Tommy
was at fault. He was of the opinion that Amanda had been emotionally
neglected by her uncaring husband. A woman needed a degree of adulation
and appreciation but Mr. Carmody had been lacking in that department.
He cited Tommy's habit of reading Chomsky in bed instead of attending
to his wife's emotional needs. She was no more than an ornament in his
life. Tommy was a typical self-centered academic, always with his nose
in a book. He did not understand that a woman needs a bit of glitz and
glamour. She needs to be seen in the casino, in the cocktail bar, in the
holiday resort in Langkawi. A beautiful young wife is like a diamond that
has little value unless it is seen and admired. Amanda was the victim of
neglect. It was a case of 'fulfillment deficit'. When a woman is not loved
in her own house, she will naturally seek solace elsewhere. The fact that
she was rewarded financially was irrelevant. Under the 'no fault' rule,
therefore, his client was entitled to claim half of her spouse's estate as well
as a reasonable monthly maintenance allowance.

During the hearing, Amanda played the part of the tragic hero. She
sobbed and sighed like a professional actor and Judge Abdul Gina seemed
unduly partial to her plight as he gazed in awe at her beautiful slim body

wrapped in a revealing red dress. His eyes almost popped out as Amanda crossed and uncrossed her long slinky legs. I got the impression, perhaps unfairly, that the judge was a dirty old man, a pervert in a privileged position to take advantage of any woman in distress. He seemed to be in total agreement with the argument being elaborated by Amanda's Counsel. He kept nodding approvingly as Raj Kumar deftly conceded that he fully appreciated the distress of the Respondent in this case. He said: 'Divorce is never easy but when a relationship has ended, the only solution is separation. You allege that your wife was unfaithful and that is a very serious charge here in Malaysia. However, in a court of law, the two most important words in the English language are 'prove it!'

Then the battle resumed in earnest as our star witness Omar Rahamat was called to the witness box. He was the janitor at the Royal Hostel on Bukit Bintang where Amanda conducted her business. He was a Pakistani national who had acquired permanent residence in Malaysia much to the displeasure of Raj Kumar, whose family had migrated from Calcutta to Selangor in 1920s and had also acquired permanent residence in what was then the Sultanate of Selangor. The hostility between the two men was evident from the start. Raj Kumar obviously looked down on janitors in general and Pakistani janitors in particular. The exchanges soon became heated as counsel and witness engaged in a bitter war of words that had its origin in centuries of hostility between the two big powers in the Subcontinent-India and Pakistan.

Omar alleged that Amanda had tipped him generously for agreeing to meet and greet her clients as he showed them to her suite on the 5th Floor. He said she normally paid him RM 100 hush money each evening for services rendered. He claimed that on her first visit she had warned him that there would be consequence if he ever mentioned her name to the authorities adding that her minder and Sudanese chauffer would pay him a visit if he betrayed her. He testified that one or two gentlemen arrived at an appointed time each evening and his task was to greet them and escort them unobtrusively to Amanda's suite. He said it was clear that she and her visitors were engaged in 'bunga bunga'.[8] It was common knowledge that 'professional' women offered sexual favours to men in mohair suits with deep pockets. Every dog on the street knew the score. It was happening every evening all over the city. KL was becoming the fun capital of Southeast Asia.

In responding, Raj Kumar then took the chainsaw to our star witness. In words oozing with scorn, he suggested that Omar was in his words 'a born liar, utterly corrupt-a man who would sell his mother for two rupees.' Clearly, his testimony was inadmissible on the grounds that all janitors were lying bastards. They would say that black was white if somebody greased their palm. Infidelity required incontrovertible proof of intimate sexual activity. No such evidence had been adduced. In fact, there was not an iota of solid proof of immoral conduct on Amanda's part.

Having listened to the evidence on both sides, Judge Abdul Gani concluded that Omar's testimony was null and void. He had not produced a single shred of hard evidence that Amanda was prostituting herself. At that point Mr. Tan knew that the case was in deep water and he 'applied for a direction', that is, he asked the judge to throw the case out. Judge Abdul Gani agreed and he granted Amanda a Decree of Divorce pursuant to Section 5 of the 1994 Act. In this case, the no fault rule would apply. He directed that the family home be sold within three months and the proceeds to be divided 50:50 between the parties. He directed no order as to maintenance since the Respondent (me) undertook to assume sole custody of the child, Leanne, whose name he repeatedly mispronounced as 'Leenie'. Furthermore, the parties would execute Deeds of Waiver. Amanda left the court smiling. She got what she wanted, a very large sum of money and the freedom to re-enter the marriage stakes with a view to further conquests. However, neither she nor I knew about my astute attorney's B plan which she promised to share with me the very next day. Amanda, for all her wiles, was no match for Ms. Ratnam.

My Counsel, Mr. Tan, told me that it was almost impossible to prove infidelity in Malaysia since the law required that the illicit sex act had to be observed and recorded by two independent witnesses. The persons involved had to be caught in flagrante delicto.[9] I still recall his parting words: 'Sorry, old boy. This is Malaysia.' I knew that within days I would receive a copy of the judicial order and terms of the settlement. What worried me most was the order to sell the family home and the proceeds to be divided 50:50 between the parties. After all, it was my villa and its market value was stated to be RM 1.2 million. And that is the story of a day in my life that changed everything. I shall say no more.'

It was midday as we left the old colonial courthouse and Mr. Tan invited to lunch at the Royal Selangor Club, on the other side of Merdeka Square. He was a member, of course, and a keen cricket connoisseur. The RSC (in Malaysia one always uses shorthand) is a splendid old building which serves amazing Malaysian, Chinese and Indian food in a tranquil setting overlooking the cricket grounds. There we dined in style off char kway teow [10] washed down with Tiger beer. Mr. Tan talked about the tension between the Chinese and Malays but he seemed assured that things were improving on that issue as both sides were enjoying a booming Malaysian economy. Suddenly, he whispered in my ear: 'My God! Look who is entering the holy of holies?' You must have guessed. Of course, it was none other than Amanda accompanied by the indubitable Raj Kumar.

After lunch, Mr. Tan had to dash back to the courthouse for his next case and Raj Kumar did likewise. As I was about to depart, Amanda beckoned me to her table and asked in a mischievous tone of voice: 'What are you doing in this den of thieves?' I almost said, 'Madam, you are the only thief here' but obviously I dare not offend the sensibilities of such a refined lady! I explained that I was a writer of sorts, seeking inspiration in a land of great mystery and natural beauty. 'Well, you've come to the right place' she, smiling seductively. She invited me to join her over coffee. In the interests of fair play, we must now hear Amanda's story. Her English was word perfect and she stated her case with surprising frankness. This is her version of things, in her own words, as best as I can recall.

'In some ways, I suppose I am a bitch-mean, nasty, malicious and spiteful. I tend to bad mouth the people I dislike and I delight is speaking ill of males in general. And why not. The male is such a dickhead-assertive, abusive, dominating and vain. In both Christianity and Islam, the male is placed on a pedestal, lording it over all creation and in his chauvinistic mind, women are a mere appendage, for man's use and benefit. They just want to ride every pretty woman they see. I have yet to meet a man who does not think through his penis.

Today Tommy has become my 'ex'-something to brag about at the club! He is basically a good bloke, but of course being an academic he'd bore you to tears with his views on language change, regional accents and the emergence of 'New English' in Malaysia and Southeast Asia. He failed to understand that a woman does not give tuppence about such matters. He is kind and considerate but he lacks passion. A woman wants to be swept off her feet by a hot-blooded Romeo and drink the cup of love to the dregs. That is not Tommy Carmody. He is a timid little mouse who begs for cheese instead of taking it by charm and guile. He is utterly 'old school', straight out of Mr. Chips. He speaks like a book and says things like: 'Gosh! what a wicked world we are living in.!' He should have been a frigging monk.

People often ask me why I walked out on Tommy. He's such a gentleman, they say, the ideal husband, refined, academic, good looking and a brilliant conversationalist. They do not know that Tommy is basically a slob. What can one do with a man who wears a hacking jacket, faded slacks and Hush Puppies? He would wear the same pair of shoes until they were worn out and only then would he buy a new pair. During his long vacation he'd head off to the rainforest in Sumatra, not with me but with his ecological friends and they'd go native for weeks on end. Last year, they went to the Himalayas and climbed half way up Annapurna [11] What a frigging waste of time! So, you see that Tommy and I were poles apart. I was starved of attention and the good life that every woman wants. He was always walking away from me, madly in love with the 'exotic' culture of the ulu people.[12] He failed to understand the oriental woman. He failed to understand that we are gold diggers.

Early in life I realized that that the only reality in life is money. The sexiest thing about a man is his money. I did not marry Tommy. I married his money. He was earning RM 12,000 a month at the university and he was raking in money big time for his English language publications. He was offered a very attractive consultation position with the Ministry of Education, in support of the government's language policy, but he refused it, saying he would not work for a corrupt government. Oh yes, my Tommy was a man of high moral principles but KL is a jungle where you sell your soul for hard cash. I was well in with UMNO and together we could have hit the jackpot but Tommy would not play ball. That's the problem with academics, they always back the opposition, the losers, the men with no balls. Money is power. The more money you have, the more powerful you become. It is that simple. And when you are really rich and utterly corrupt, the government will confer on you the title Datin,[13] so that you can join the club and fuck everybody. Women generally do not have the brain power to create wealth by means of enterprise. So, they have to use other strategies in order to come between a man and his money. Divorce is one such effective strategy, much invoked by feminists. The 'no fault' rule means that every whore can now relieve her man of half his estate. Look, let's be frank. All professional people are whores-lawyers, politicians, footballers and so on. We all charge substantial fees for our services. We fuck our clients. In fact, prostitution is the more honourable profession in that the client usually gets value for his money. OK, I cheated a bit on Tommy. But it was for a good cause. And in the court, I got the judge onside. That was easy. A woman with good legs and firm breasts can cast a spell on any Family Law judge. I could see the lust in his eyes. Body language does not lie. He wanted to put his finger in the jam pot. Sure, he can have a ride any time as long as he hands me hard cash. It's a funny old world we're living in. Really, life's a bitch. Have I made my point of view clear?'

Amanda had indeed made her point of view abundantly clear. In fact, at the end of our interview she gave me her business card in case I should ever need a massage. Some days later, I met Tommy again. He told me that Ms. Ratnam had put before him a very attractive proposition. In brief, she advised him to do a runner. She advised him to sell the villa in Bangsar forthwith and relocate to any one of a dozen countries in Southeast Asia that were screaming out for professionals like Tommy with years of expertise in Applied Linguistics and Language Education. Furthermore, she advised him to exchange his British passport for an Irish one, since he was both a British subject and an Irish national. That way, he could disappear without a trace. At that time in KL a lot of illicit money was flowing into luxury real estate and secret buyers in many countries were keen to get their hand on high-end properties. There was no requirement for real estate agents to disclose the names of either sellers or buyers. Ms. Ratnam could easily dispose of Tommy's villa and nobody would be the wiser.

Tommy discovered that several countries in Southeast Asia were actively recruiting university lecturers, the most promising being Vietnam, where all of the 40 universities in that country were desperately trying to recruit English language specialists. During the mid-semester break at his university in KL, he flew to Hanoi where he was interviewed and offered a position as Senior Lecturer at the National University there. On his return to KL, he began the tedious task of packing his belongings in trunks for shipment to Hanoi. Meanwhile the sale of his villa was proceeding in the capable hands of Ms. Ratnam who was well versed in negotiating confidential deals behind closed doors. I had to leave KL at the end of that week but I learned that Tommy and Leanne had successfully relocated to Vietnam.

I also learned that Amanda was incandescent with rage when she discovered that she had been outwitted by Ms. Ratnam. I was told that she had left KL and had gone to Singapore where she married an American banker. As my good friend Abdul Rahman put it, 'another lamb, or should I say a randy old ram, to the slaughter. She will set him up with a sexy young Indonesian babe and then sue for divorce on the grounds of infidelity. And if it works out as planned, she will receive her share of his penthouse apartment on Orchard Road, currently valued at $2.5 million. After that, the sky is the limit.'

I expect that both Tommy and Amanda each found fulfillment in their new situation. As Shakespeare said: All's well that ends well.

END NOTES:

1   *Liberties*: An area of Dublin city that was once outside the municipal boundary and allowed to preserve its own jurisdiction (hence 'liberties'). A historic working-class area.

2   *gurrier*: an ill-mannered loutish person from a poor part of Dublin; the word is possibly derived from 'gur-cake,' a cheap confection often associated with children from deprived families. For more on its origin, see Dolan (2006). *A Dictionary of Hiberno English*. p.116

3   *hantu*: The Malay word for spirits or the 'undead'

4   *Pontianak*: The blood-sucking vampire of Malaysia folklore who appears young and beautiful in order to attract male victims.

5   *UMNO*: United Malays National Organization-the anchor party of the coalition that ruled Malaysia from Independence until 2018 when it lost power to the Pakatan Harapan (PH) coalition.

6   *craic:* The Irish word for high-spirited conversation and jollity

7   *Chindian:* a person of mixed race, half Chinese and half Indian

8   *bunga bunga:* sexual activity. Originally a tribal ritual of sexual abandon.

9   *in flagrante delicto:* caught in the act; often referring to sexual activity

10   *char kway teow:* flat rice noodles, stir-fried with Chinese sausage, garlic, chili, oyster sauce, fish cake and dark soy sauce.

11   *Annapurna:* A section of the Himalayas in Nepal.

12   *ulu:* The indigenous people of Borneo

13   *Datin:* In Malaysia, a title of respect bestowed on a meritorious woman.

THE LAST RESIDENT

Clive Bonner-Davies was the last Resident[1] of Sandakan when Sabah was known as British North Borneo[2] and administered by the Chartered Company before the Japanese invasion in January 1942. He was a gentleman and a scholar; a man of immaculate manners and good breeding, a graduate of Oxford University where he read Greats[3] and graduated with the degree BA summa cum laude. He joined the Foreign Service and worked in London for some years before being sent to his first posting, the Cape of Good Hope. He obviously impressed the Foreign Office and in due course he was promoted to First Secretary at the High Commission in Blantyre. On his return to London, he was approached by the Chartered Company and offered the position of Resident in Sandakan. Clive was moving up in the world and he did not hesitate in accepting the new post in British North Borneo.

One had to admit that Clive was ambassadorial material. His parents were wealthy merchants in Bath and he was an only child. At the tender age of 12 he was sent to Eton where he excelled not only at his studies but also at cricket. He was a consummate all-rounder, equally adept with the bat or ball. Academically, he was top of his form and he consistently scored 'A' grades. Not surprisingly, he was chosen as dux of Form 6. At Oxford, he decided to take up Sanskrit so that he could gain an insight into the great culture of the Indian subcontinent. He felt that one day he would be called on to serve the Crown in some remote corner of the British Empire and as an empire builder and dispenser of British civility, it was fitting and proper that he should possess a knowledge of classical languages. He spoke RP [4]-not the reduced version that one heard on the BBC but the real thing, as described by Professor Daniel Jones. He had a keen ear for regional accents and he could accurately place a person anywhere in Britain or Ireland by their accent. Some said that Clive was so old-fashioned and eccentric that the Foreign Office had banished him to the last outpost of the British Empire, North Borneo. That was probably an unfair assessment since Borneo was of great economic and strategic importance. It had vast natural resources-oil, rubber, tea, tobacco, hardwoods and manganese and of course, it was a vital link in the chain of British colonies, in an area that was contested by other empire builders-the Dutch, Portuguese and Spanish. Clive looked and spoke like an ambassador and he saw his post as Resident as having ambassadorial status. His mystique was considerably enhanced by the fact that he was happily divorced. His ex-wife had run off with a German geologist from Windhoek in South West Africa. Good riddance. She was a real pain, full of horse manure and an ego as big as her behind. He should have known better. Her grandparents were Scottish Presbyterians and that should have rung a bell. He was not himself particularly religious but described himself as Anglo-Catholic.

He loved Cape Town. What a wonderful place-'the fairest cape in all the world'. He and his young wife Sophie used to explore the Great Karoo, the Kalahari and South West Africa. It was in Windhoek that Sophie met the charming Fritz von Kühn, a small stout man with large handlebar moustaches. He and Sophie fell hopelessly in love and it was not long before the ugly prospect of divorce arose. The separation was a shock when it came but all things considered, Clive was much relieved. Naturally, he regarded Fritz 'of the long whiskers' as a Nazi posing as a geologist. He hoped and fully expected that Sophie would be the bane of his life.

Clive was a good six foot tall, with broad shoulders and an agile body. His face was tanned from his years in Africa and his pale blue eyes lit up a face that seemed carved out of granite. His dark wavy hair was brushed back and threads of silver had begun to appear in it, adding a certain gravitas to his overall appearance. Nothing showed his class more than this dress code. He made no concession to the tropical heat and kept alive a long tradition of British sartorial elegance-dinner jacket, black tie, smoking jacket, pin-striped suits, all made to measure by his bespoke tailor in Jermyn Street. He was a man of sober habits in all things. Some would say that he was a grey character, quite 'old school', even Victorian, completely out of kilter with the mores of a liberal progressive age. For instance, he always dressed for dinner even when alone; he knew how to eat his soup and he ate his peas with a knife and fork.

Clive was concerned at his ever-expanding girth. He adhered to the strictest of diets but in spite of his monastic lifestyle and sober habits, he was barely able to get into a pair of size 46 trousers. He did his beach run every morning and he played tennis every Friday morning. He swam 20 lengths of the Residency pool at sunset but still he continued to gain weight. He was a man of habit, up at the crack of dawn when he would head for the beach and do a five-mile jog, followed by his panting footman-cum-butler, Moses, who carried his towel, drinking water, cigars and diary. At the end of the beach, he would halt, sit on a log and light up a cigar.

'Tell me Moses, what's going on in that inscrutable head of yours?'

'Well, Sir Clive, looks like you have busy day ahead. Staff meeting at ten and lunch with the District Officer at 10.30'

'My God! Lunch with the D.O. did you say? Cancel that. Why waste precious time with that old windbag?'

'Very good, sir. May I remind you that you promised to call on the Rev. Hollingsworth at St. Paul's this week. Shall I confirm that?"

'Now, that's more like it. A man of some scholarship and a connoisseur of good wine.'

'Then, cricket in the afternoon. The Cavaliers versus the crew of the Enterprise.'

'That should be fun. Jolly good show.'

'Dinner at 7 p.m. as usual. I take it you are dining alone, sir.'

'Not quite. I've invited the new chap, Sadler and his wife. Can't say I'm looking forward to it. The price one pays…'

'What shall I tell the chef, sir? Nothing too oriental, I expect.'

'Precisely. Keep it simple. Good old roast beef and Yorkshire pudding, followed by crème caramel and a cheese board. And two bottles of Cabernet Merlot.'

Back in the Residency, Clive had breakfast alone. He breakfasted off porridge, toast and two duck eggs. The eggs had to be soft but not runny. If the eggs were too soft or too hard, he flew into a rage and hurled abuse at the chef, Kumar Dev. Then, he looked over the morning papers. Staff members arrived at 8.30 a.m. and the Residency opened promptly at 9 a.m. Clive was a stickler for decorum and dress code-no flashy ties, no suede shoes, no short dresses, no pink shirts and no long hair. One had to maintain British standards of decency. Let the natives dress up in their lemon-green pyjamas and sarongs and their hideous gay headwear. That was their prerogative but British officials had to act and dress in a manner appropriate to their membership of the Chartered Company. There must be no effusive greetings or close proximity to visitors; at all times there must be stiff upper lip and formal etiquette. Visitors must know that it was considered bad form to disagree with any comment made by the Resident. The correct response to whatever he proposed was: 'Absolutely so, sir!'

The Resident's first task each day was reading and responding to cables and mail. The second secretary, Peter Ashton, would have opened all the mail and sorted it in order of importance, marking important points in red ink. Then, Clive would call him in and tell him how to respond to any matters needing a response. The standard response to queries and complaints was as follows: 'We have noted the concern(s) you raised in your letter of (date) and we assure you that the matter is receiving top priority. You will be hearing from us in due course.' When you saw the words 'top priority' you knew that your letter had gone straight into the waste paper basket. At ten o'clock, there would be a briefing with the Consul, or the first secretary, or the cultural officer or the military attaché, or the education office, or the new developmental officer responsible for native affairs. The one thing that everyone liked about Clive was that he had no favourites. Everyone got a fair crack of the whip. Of course, all recommendations and projects had to be vetted by the Governor General, before being approved.

Clive was quite happy in his role as Resident. His own political views coincided with the colonial mind-set. Under the British colonial system, the country was divided into Residencies and subdivided into Districts. Initially, there were only two Residencies, the East Coast with headquarters at Sandakan and the West Coast with headquarters at Jesselton. In 1922, new Residencies were created in Kudat, Tawau and Interior. The Chartered Company had developed an elaborate bureaucracy for dealing with the natives. Under the Residency system, British officials held the top posts while native chiefs managed people at grassroots level. Each Residency was divided into a small number of Districts and each District was managed by a District Officer, who was British and worked in close co-ordination with the Resident. The D.O was in effect the head of the local civil service, responsible for law enforcement, tax collection, distribution of welfare benefits, education and health provisions and developmental projects. Clive subscribed to the notion of white rule. 'White rule means right rule.' North Borneo had been acquired by the Chartered Company through a series of concessions obtained from the Sultan of Sulu in 1882. The Chartered Company was successful because it adopted the age-old British policy of 'divide and rule' and race-based policies. It was a neo-feudal elite-led body of wise men, dispensing British governance and requiring absolute loyalty from its subjects. The colonial mind-set was clearly expressed by Warnford-Lock (1907):[5] 'By nature, the Malay is an idler, the Chinaman is a thief, and the Indian is a drunkard. Yet, each, in his own class of work is both cheap and efficient when properly supervised.' As Farish Noor (2010:72) [6] observes, colonial policy was based on the British perception of racial supremacy, the imperialist notion of 'paternalistic duty' and 'the white man's burden' towards the coloured races, as well as the colonial-capitalist notion of the Malays as 'lazy natives' who required Western supervision. Hence, the state's administration and coffers must remain forever in the safe hands of an enlightened and honest British administration. The majority race, the Malays, were given certain privileges and Islam was accepted as the state religion, with scant regard for the rights of non-Malay minorities, especially the Christian Kadazan, Dusun, Rungus and Murut people. Unlike Sarawak, where the White Rajah[7] won the hearts and minds of the natives, the North Borneo administration remained aloof, paternalistic and Malay-centric.

The Chartered Company regarded all natives as dishonest, scheming and corrupt and hence elaborate measures were put in place to ensure honest dealing. It was assumed that all natives were liars and cheats and that every penghulu (headman), policeman and civil servant was out to rip off the system. Hence, the Public Service Department (PSD) imposed sclerotic rules and procedures-a veritable maze of red tape. The state controlled every aspect of life. One had to obtain permission to leave the state, to move house, to marry, to avail of state schooling, to open a business, the sell a property or land, to visit a forest reserve, to shoot game or to employ foreign workers. For example, in order to receive medical treatment in a government clinic or hospital, one had first to obtain a Letter of Undertaking from the Health Department. That was not a simple matter. The application had to be made in triplicate, in English, on the prescribed form, together with a covering letter addressed to the Honourable Head of Department, together with a number of supporting documents, such as a copy of one's identity card, a certificate of religion, as well as the name and address of one's employer or sponsor. You had to know your File Number and process your claim in the correct sequence, moving from office A, to office B, to office C on different floors and sometimes in different buildings. In that way, people would spend days wandering about the various government offices, processing various claims or seeking various permissions. The most difficult of all departments was Finance. Getting money out of Finance was like getting blood out of a stone. That was how it had to be in a land plagued by tribal tensions, lawlessness, chaos and corruption.

Clive had grave reservations about the competence and suitability of his new developmental officer, Simon Sadler. He was shocked when the young man appeared for his dinner appointment in casual dress and an open-neck shirt. He made allowance for his wife, Gloria, since she was American and American females said and did the most outlandish things. It did not help when Simon asked:

'Why do you dress up for dinner? Isn't that rather superfluous in Borneo?'

'I do not dress up for dinner' replied Clive. 'I dress for dinner.'

He noticed that his new assistant failed to add the little word 'sir'. Things went from bad to worse. The Sadlers did not know how to eat their soup and Gloria kept saying that the food was 'super'. Clive was not amused. My God, what was the world coming to? The new officer was supposedly educated but he had never heard of the Oxford 'Greats'. Clive was no snob and he did not mind people joining the Foreign Service with degrees from red-brick universities as long as they knew some Latin or Greek or some oriental language. He did not mind people speaking in regional accents, even though he winced when Gloria kept saying that everything was 'cool'. One had to make allowance for Americans, of course. Was it not Oscar Wilde who remarked 'America is the only country that went from barbarism to decadence without civilization in between'? But surely a person wishing to join the British diplomatic service should at least speak the King's English. Naturally, Clive would have preferred people of his own kind, the cream of British society, old boys of Eaton, Winchester and Harrow-thoroughly decent chaps who graduated from Oxbridge, or St. Andrews or Trinity College Dublin. How could the Foreign Office recruit someone who had never heard of, much less studied Cicero or Virgil. What was he to do with a man whose only claim to fame was a degree in sociology from the University of Essex? It was simply preposterous to send him an assistant whose only ambition in life was to 'explore native culture'. He did not need an anthropologist; he needed an able administrator who would help him to discharge his many and onerous duties in a state that was just emerging from head-hunting.

In Europe, the political situation was looking ominous. Herr Hitler was on the move and no doubt his partners in crime, the Japanese, would launch an offensive in Southeast Asia but Clive was not unduly concerned. The war cabinet in London was fully aware of the Japanese menace but North Borneo had no reason to be apprehensive since the Japanese would never get past Fortress Singapore. Besides, plans were under way to bolster Borneo's defences with Anzac troops and military hardware.

Clive, therefore, relaxed and turned his attention to the other great love in his live, cricket.

Cricket was one of the hallmarks of the British civility, exported from the playing fields of the public schools to the Indian subcontinent, Australia and New Zealand. For British people, it was part and parcel of the glory that was the British Empire. It was, along with church services, military parades, tiffin and garden parties, an essential component of colonial life. Cricket left an indelible mark on the collective consciousness of the colonials. What could be more inspiring than a group of men attired in white flannels playing a genteel game 'under the alien sky' watched by adoring devotees of both sexes, the men elegantly attired in boaters and their club blazers; the ladies flaunting their summer frocks and straw hats. Cricket was the badge of class. Lesser mortals played horrid games such as baseball, rounders, hurling and shinty, but no stick game had the grace and beauty of cricket. It built character and team spirit; the test team built national pride like no other game. It taught one manners. There was no talking back to the umpire, or waving of the arms or stamping on the ground. If you were out, you were out. If the umpire was unsure, you walked. Honour was more important than winning.

Clive was most aggrieved when rumblings of war reached Borneo in the late 30s. 'Damn Hitler and the Japs,' he was heard to say 'the blighters are going to interrupt our annual war with the men Down Under. 'Unfortunately, the war came to Borneo sooner than anyone else had expected. The Battle of North Borneo [8] interrupted not only the cricket calendar but the whole geo-political map of the region. Clive had seen it coming. In a series of dispatches to the Governor General, he predicted the Japanese onslaught on Southeast Asia. According to Clive, a great new global empire was there for the taking. The Tripartite Pact between the Axis Powers of Germany, Italy and Japan would change the map of the world. The Germans would rule Europe and the Japanese would rule Asia. They would divide the Middle East between them. Yes, the British Empire was about to be wound up. Fortunately for the West, Hitler decided to invade Russia-a massive error and the Japanese bombed Pearl Harbour in December 1941, bringing the United States into the war. Of course, neither the Governor nor the war cabinet in London took Clive's analysis of the situation seriously. They believed that the Japanese would never get past Fortress Singapore.

Clive knew better and he began making contingency plans for the Battle of North Borneo. He was hoping to evacuate his staff to a safe haven, such as Labuan but he soon discovered that the Japanese were everywhere. The only cover was the interior and that was forest. However, one could live off the fruits of the forest if all else failed. He, therefore, drilled his staff in jungle survival tactics and dispatched them in groups to the interior. Nobody knows how many of them survived. What we do know is that those who remained in Sandakan were interned by the Japanese and any known British officers were taken out and shot. It is widely assumed that Clive was one the first POWs to be executed. Three batches of POWs were made to march all the way from Sandakan to Ranau on the infamous death marches. [9]

The West had won a glorious victory but the war graves at Sandakan, Kundasang and Labuan should serve to remind everyone that nobody really wins a war. Clive Bonner-Davies, the last Resident of Sandakan did not abandon his sinking ship. He bravely held on to the bitter end as one would expect from an English gentleman raised on the playing fields of Eton.

ENDNOTES:

1   *Resident:* A British government agent in a semi-independent state. In Malaya, the Resident effectively ruled the state and kept the peace while at the same time creating the myth that the state belonged to the Malays. Residents adopted a 'divide and rule' policy whereby some Malays were accepted into government while leaving commerce to the Chinese, estate management to the Indians and leaving the indigenous people to their own devices.

2   *British North Borneo:* In 1881, Alfred Dent formed the British North Borneo Association and obtained a royal charter the same year. In 1882, in a series of shady deals, the Chartered Company bought the territory now known as Sabah from its former owners, the Sultan of Sulu and the Sultan of Brunei. In 1888, North Borneo became a protectorate of Great Britain, but its administration remained entirely in the hands of the Chartered Company. For 64 years, (1882-1946) the Chartered Company ran the country quite successfully.

3   *Greats* (Literae Humaniores): The honours course in classics, philosophy and ancient history at Oxford University.

4   *RP: Received Pronunciation:* The standard form of British English pronunciation, based on educated speech in Southern England. See Peter Roach (1992:89): *Introducing Phonetics.*

5   C. G. *Warnford-Lock* (1907). *Mining in Malaya for Gold and Tin.* London: Crowther & Goodman (pp.31-32). A guidebook written for the benefit of British colonial corporate managers.

6   *Farish A. Noor* (2010). *What Your Teacher Didn't Tell You .* Vol.1. Petaling Jaya: Mata Hari.

7   *The White Rajah:* The Brooke Raj in Sarawak. In 1839, James Brooke set out intending to sail his schooner, The Royalist, to North Borneo where he hoped to establish a trading station. He arrived in Sarawak just in time to quell a rebellion by the local Malays against the Raja Muda of Brunei. In an unprecedented gesture of goodwill, the Sultan of Brunei ceded Sarawak to James Brooke. See W. Reece (1993). *The Name of Brooke.*

8   *Battle of North Borneo:* In 1941, Borneo became a prime target of the Japanese Imperial forces. Its 35th Infantry Brigade was charged with the annexation of Borneo-both the British protectorates of North Borneo, Sarawak and Brunei

and Dutch East Indies (Kalimantan). On December 15, 1941, the Japanese forces captured both Miri and Seria with very little resistance from the British forces. By the end of December, they had taken Brunei, Labuan and Jesselton. In January 1942, using small fishing boats they landed at Sandakan. The North Borneo Armed Constabulary with only 650 men offered little resistance. Next day, the Governor, Charles Robert Smith, surrendered and was interned with other staff. Sandakan became a prisoner of war camp for over 2,700 Anzac and British POWs, transported there after the fall of Singapore.

9   *death marches*: After the fall of Singapore in 1942, the Japanese transferred some 2,700 Allied POWs to a large prison camp in Sandakan. In January, 1945, after living for three long years in captivity, in appalling conditions, on starvation rations, the Japanese decided to move 455 of the fittest POWs to Jesselton to act as coolie labourers. They had to cover a distance of 260 km over rough terrain, jungle and mountain passes. The emaciated servicemen were kicked and beaten and half of them succumbed to dysentery and ill-treatment. Eventually, the survivors reached the small town of Ranau where they had to halt owing to Allied air activity over the Western region and Jesselton. There, they all died of disease or starvation. The Kundasang War Memorial commemorates this tragic event. The Ranau death march was one of the horror stories of World War 2. (See: www.sandekan-deathmarch.com)

EYE OF THE TIGER

Ignacio Tupak lived with his parents and three sisters in a single-storey bamboo house beside the Papar river in the foothills of the Crocker Range. There were many remote villages there in the Penampang[1] District of Sabah. It is very scenic country on the edge of the rainforest overlooking the South China Sea. The Tupaks were Kadazans, just like their cousins, the Dusun who lived higher up the mountain. They were the original indigenous people of Sabah, who managed to live off the fruits of the forest and rice farming. Although no strangers to poverty, the hill tribes were a happy people, for the most part Christian. They spoke their own Kadazan-Dusun language and kept alive their ancient traditions, especially the Harvest Festival. They were industrious and jolly with a Latin temperament, quite distinct from the other races of East Malaysia.

Ignacio was the youngest of the Tupak family. Everyone called him Iggy. He had three sisters, all older and wiser than him. He got on well with the eldest sister, Emily, who looked after him, made sure his school uniform was spanking clean, packed his school bag and tied his shoe laces. However, the two other girls often teased him. They called him a spoiled brat and a dirty little liar. The problem was that Iggy's imagination was bigger than his boots. He would turn an ordinary incident into a dramatic event. He was very fond of animals. He had a dog, two cats, a monitor lizard and a bowl of six goldfish. He preferred animals to people and certainly more than his two silly sisters, who spent their time dressing up and showing off their embroidered dresses and beaded hair. He was much happier talking to his animals.

Iggy's fondness for animals and insects had something to do with his mother, Monica, who used to read bedtime stories to the children. She would read the stories out of a big book with lots of colour illustrations-stories such as 'The Fox and the Crow', 'The Three Billy Goats Gruff', 'The Very Hungry Caterpillar', etc. For Iggy, those stories were as real as the animals that lived on the farms and in the forest. Animals made more sense to him than humans possibly because from his perspective, they gave love without demanding it; they had teeth, but they do not bite unless you abused them. Moreover, they are free and indifferent. They do not know the meaning of obligation and they can get by with a minimum vocabulary. He saw nothing implausible in a pink elephant playing a piano or a tiger making a stew out of bread and cheese, or a barking deer riding a bicycle. Whatever the cause, it was clear that Iggy preferred animals to people who for the most part tended to be irrational, gross and demanding and rejected magic. In Sabah, one was surrounded by magic. The jungle was home to all sorts of 'hantu'-mischievous spirits that had to be respected and appeased. He always fastened his bedroom window at night in case a 'hungry ghost' came looking for food. He believed that in the rainforest, you never walked alone. When you stopped to urinate in the forest, you kowtowed to the tree so as not to offend the 'hantu' lurking in the branches. Of course, his sisters only laughed at all this silly nonsense. However, they too knew that the jungle was a living cosmos, home to snakes, monkeys, bearded boar and deadly red ants. As for 'hantu' lurking in the trees, steams, pools and dense undergrowth, all that was folklore. Only silly boys like Iggy believed in 'hantu', just as some children believe in fairies. That was what their English teacher, Miss O'Connor, told them. And she never lied. She was a Catholic.

Every morning the children were up at the crack of dawn. The Tupaks lived in Kampung Tiku and the nearest school was at Kampung Buayan, a good six miles away. They would walk along the dirt track that connected the two villages. It took them a good hour to reach the community school, a low wooden building on stilts, just like the longhouses in which the village people lived. Before setting out on their long trek to school, their mother would sprinkle them with holy water to ward off the evil one. The children often sang a traditional Kadazan song as they marched along the dirt trail in single file, the way ducks follow their leader across marsh land.

The air was pure and bracing and the jungle was alive with living things – pitcher plants, giant orchids, lotus flowers and the beautiful but foul-smelling Rafflesia.[2] Fruit trees abounded-fig, mango, banana, mangosteen and durian. Figs attracted hornbills and as well as long-tailed monkeys. In the distance one could hear the loud hooting of the gibbon, known locally as 'wak-wak'. There were also larger animals, such as the bearded boar, barking deer and the formidable black water buffalo. However, there are no tigers in Sabah. There are tigers in the wild in the northern states of peninsular Malaysia but even there, their numbers have diminished and they end up in pharmacies where their body parts are reduced to tablets believed to boost virility.

Miss O'Connor told the children that Penampang was the Garden of Eden and perhaps it was. She never lied, unlike cheeky little Iggy. All the village people went to church on Sunday. For them, God was in His Heaven and all was right with the world. They could not understand why people would choose to live in a concrete jungle like Jesslelton, as Kota Kinabalu was known in those days. They could not understand why the government was clearing the jungle and planting the land-their traditional land-with horrid palm oil trees. They hated to see their sacred forest being violated by logging companies that cut down the ancient hardwoods and transported the mighty logs down the Papar River for export to Singapore and West Malaysia. Miss O'Connor explained that all of that enterprise was being done in the name of 'development' and even though nobody in the mountain villages really understood the concept of 'rural development', they accepted that it must be a good thing since Miss O'Connor said it was. And she never lied. She said the palm oil plantations would bring prosperity to Sabah. Young Kadazan and Dusun men could find work on the plantations and earn a dollar or two a day. Now, that was real money. Then they could save up, buy a motorbike and ride off to Papar or Jesselton to enjoy the good life. At morning assembly, Miss O'Connor read a passage from the Bible, pausing after each verse, which was translated into Kadazan. Then, they all sang a hymn, praising God for the paradise that was Penampang.

As the children were passing a clearing in the forest, Iggy noticed an awesome butterfly, the biggest he had ever seen. It was the magnificent Rajah Brooke Birdwing [3] with its distinctive black and green wings and bright red head. Iggy had never seen this rare and beautiful butterfly. It flew from plant to plant flapping its dazzling electric green wings. He followed it across a patch of bamboo grass but the butterfly read his mind and made off to a thicket beyond his reach. Iggy sat down in the long grass hoping that the butterfly would return. Suddenly, he sensed something moving in the long grass. Through the long shoots, he saw two amber eyes peering in his direction. It was undoubtedly a tiger-a real live Malaysian tiger.[4] Iggy knew instinctively that it would be unwise to run away. No human can outpace a tiger. As it came closer, he noticed the tiger's white muzzle, the blotches of white above it eyes, its yellow-ochre coat with black stripes, its white belly and its short-muscled forelegs with long retractable claws. It was, in any man's language, an awesome sight. The tiger showed no signs of aggression as it inched closer to the boy. Iggy was stunned, not knowing what to expect. He had been told there were no tigers in Sabah but here he was staring into the eyes of a tiger. The tiger stared back at him and moved closer. Then it began sniffing the boy and as a token of friendship began licking Iggy's feet. He always walked barefoot to school. Iggy patted the animal and then it sat down beside him. He continued patting the tiger. It seemed to enjoy the experience and rolled over on its back showing its white belly. Iggy thought that the poor animal might be hungry so he took out his hunch box and shared his ham sandwiches with the tiger. They both ate greedily. They seemed to sense that they were kindred spirits and Iggy knew how to talk to animals. In fact, the tiger looked as lost as Iggy and seemed to crave company. They just sat there in an act of mutual bonding. Then it suddenly dawned on Iggy that he should be on his way to school, so be bid farewell to the tiger, which wandered off into the bamboo grass, looking rather sad. Iggy headed back to the dirt track to rejoin his sisters. But he got lost in the long grass and wandered aimlessly this way and that, utterly lost in the wilderness.

It was not until they reached the school that his sisters discovered that 'little brat' had gone missing. They feared that he might have been abducted by the 'hantu'. Miss O'Connor lost no time in forming a search party and armed with parangs and long bamboo sticks, they scampered off into the lush green padi fields towards the river. Miss O'Connor kept blowing her netball whistle and the children called out: "Iggy! Iggy! Where are you, Iggy?" The din was too much for the birds and monkeys and they left their feeding haunts in fear and dread. Much to their relief, they soon found Iggy in the long grass, his shoes slung over his shoulder and his school uniform looking none too clean. 'What have you been up, Master Ignatio?' boomed the stern voice of Miss O'Connor. 'Please Miss, I seen a beautiful butterfly and I followed it into the jungle. And there I came face to face with a tiger, a real Malaysian tiger.'

'Did you now?' she replied in a scornful tone of voice. Of course, nobody believed Iggy's story and all the children chanted in chorus: 'There are no tigers in Sabah.' They said that he probably saw a civet, or a 'kuching besar' (big cat). But Iggy insisted that it was an awesome Malayan tiger and that he looked into the eyes of the tiger and the tiger stared back at him, and then he and tiger sat side by side. He said he had shared his lunch with the tiger, showing his empty lunch box. Once more Miss O'Connor asked the boy: 'Are you telling the truth because if you are not, I will redden your bottom with my rattan cane.' Iggy did not flinch. 'Honest to God, Miss. I really saw and patted the tiger and as I was leaving it looked sad.'

Miss O'Connor and the pupils returned to the school and she telephoned the police to report a stray tiger in the vicinity of the school. The police officer seemed quite excited. 'That is very good news', he said. 'We have received information that a tiger cub at Lok Kawi Wildlife Park escaped and has been seen prowling in the Crocker Range. We shall send a patrol immediately.'

And so, it was the tiger cub was captured and returned to his home in the Wildlife Park. If you go to Kota Kinabalu, make sure to take a day trip to Lok Kawi Wildlife Park where you will see the tiger, Pak Belang, in his enclosure looking quite happy to be back home. And do not believe the people who tell you that there are no tigers in Sabah. Now we know that there is at least one tiger there and that's no lie.

ENDNOTES:

1   *Penampang District* is on the Crocker Range, south of Kota Kinabalu, the capital of Sabah. It is an area of incredible natural beauty on the banks of the Papar

River, with dense rainforest and paddy fields on the lower slopes. Generations of Kadazan and Dusun people have lived there for ages.

2 *Rafflesia*: A parasitic plant that bears a flaming red flower up to one metre across. It is the largest flower in the world.

3 *Tiger extract* is a much sought-after commodity in Southeast Asia as it is regarded as a cure for erectile dysfunction.

4 *Rajah Brooke Birdwing*: The rare and beautiful butterfly found in Borneo and Malaysia. Discovered by Alfred R. Wallace and named after Sir James Brooke, who was the first white Rajah of Sarawak. The wingspan is 15-17 cm.

5 Malaysian tiger: There are no tigers in Sabah. They are found mainly in Sumatra and the northern states of peninsular Malaysia. The tiger is known as Pak Belang (striped fellow) in Malay.

THE TAMARIND MAN

18

Klang[1] was once a royal town, the former capital of Selangor. It takes its name from the river which flows across the Klang Valley extending from beyond Kuala Lumpur to Port Klang on the west coast. The majestic Sultan Abdul Aziz Museum in Klang showcases the history of the Selangor Sultanate that began in 1766. However, the current Sultan of Selangor, Sultan Sharafuddin Idris Shah, no longer resides in Klang. The state capital and the Sultan's palace were moved to Shah Alam in 1974 when Selangor relinquished Kuala Lumpur (KL) to the federal government. As Kuala Lumpur and Shah Alam prospered and expanded, Klang stagnated. Today, it is no longer the most beautiful town in Malaysia. It is shabby and run down, surrounded by sprawling industrial estates.

What Klang still retains, however, is tons of old-world charm; its bustling streets are alive with people of Indian, Malay and Chinee origin going about their business in what looks like chaotic fashion, passing by age-old Indian shop houses, street markets, ancient Hainese coffee shops where the beans are roasted with butter and rows of Malay 'makan'[2] stalls serving ready-to-eat spicy meals. People travel from KL to Klang to dine in style in the many famous restaurants there such as the *Boon Tat Seafood Restaurant*. The main street in Klang, Jalan Tengku Kilana, is called Little India. It is a mile long extending from the old bridge across the Klang River to the Simpang Lima roundabout. During Deepavali [3] it is packed with shoppers from all over the Klang Valley swarming like bees around rows of garland-festooned shops which transport you to India and offer you a wonderland of exotic merchandise-authentic Indian spices,

125

pills and potions, aromatic oils, saris, silks, fashion items, silver jewellery, handicrafts and incredible Indian food served on a banana leaf.

It was in this Indian enclave, Little India, that Mohan Pillai grew up, spending most of his free time helping out in the fruit shop run by his parents on Jalan Tengku Kelana. The family lived above the shop, in a dingy two-bedroom apartment and every day was a day of toil, sorting and displaying the crates of fruit and serving an endless chain of customers who always haggled over the price of produce. They did a brisk trade in mango, guava, durian, rambutan, dragon fruit, snake fruit and longan. They did not deal in imported apples, oranges, grapes, etc since those items were sold cheaply in the many convenience stores and in the supermarkets. The Pillais traded only in organic fruits, cultivated locally and in peppercorn from Sarawak and in authentic spices imported from Java. It was hard work stocking and re-stocking the fruit crates, weighing and selling the fruit and it was not very profitable after paying rent and municipal taxes.

Mohan attended La Salle School where he received a good all-round education. It is a Mission school open to all races and religions and one of the oldest schools in Klang. In Mohan's words it was 'the place where I learned brotherhood with no colour.' Like his parents, he was a Catholic and every Sunday they went to church at St. Anne's Church in Port Klang where miracles were said to happen. Later in life, however, Mohan seldom went to church and he distanced himself from religion when he joined the local branch of the PSRM (the Malaysian Socialist Party) [4] in 1974. However, 'socialism' was a dirty word in Malaysia at that time and hundreds of active members of the Socialist Party were detained and locked up under the draconian Internal Security Act 1960 (ISA). Mohan, however, did not give up. He continued to agitate for equality, freedom of speech, freedom of assembly and an end to racism and discrimination. In 1982 he was elected to the Municipal Council where he continued his tirade against the blatant corruption, misrule and racism of the ruling BN [6] coalition. The ideology of the BN coalition is known as ketuanan Melayu (Malay supremacy) which asserts that only bumiputeras (sons of the soil) are entitled to the full range of benefits reserved for them. According to Dean Johns (2011) [7] 'successive UMNO/BN regimes have violated every principle of civic virtue and good governance in their insatiable lust for power and plunder.' He goes even further (on page 132) where he states: 'Like every other people-robbing government, Malaysia's BN regime supports its thievery with a system of corruption, repression, secrecy, lies and low cunning.'

It is hard to understand the animosity which many Malay Muslims display towards the Indian population especially in Kuala Lumpur. Whenever there is a protest by Indian workers or students over unfair treatment and discrimination, one often hears comments such as: 'Bloody Indians! Why don't they go back to their own country?' Many Indians could say they are in their own country since the parts of Malaysia known as the Straits Settlements [8] once belonged to British India. Many Indians settled in Malaysia during the colonial era. They worked as indentured labourers in the tin mining towns of Perak and on the coffee, sugar and rubber plantations in Malacca. Some English-educated Indians were appointed to more professional positions as civil servants. Most of the economic activity was in the Klang Valley and it was there that the great majority of Indians settled. In fact, a lot of Malaysia's thriving economy was achieved not by the ethnic Malays but by industrious Indians. It was Indian engineers who built KL and the roads and railways across the country.

Mohan's parents were Tamils who were fluent speakers of Tamil, Malay and English. Their parents settled in Malaysia during the colonial era. However, they were always regarded as being racially inferior and were fully accepted only if they 'crossed the river', that is, if they converted to Islam. The Pillais had no intention of ever 'crossing the river'. The just wanted to live in peace and harmony with all Malaysians irrespective of race, religion or political affiliation.

However, in the early 80s there was a good deal of racial tension between the Malays and the Indians in the Klang Valley, especially in Kuala Lumpur and Shah Alam. It looked as if the ruling BN regime was out to provoke the Indians by a spate of derogatory racist comments and hate-filled speeches. There were heated exchanges in the Klang Municipal Council when a BN member called Mohan and his followers 'socialist subversives' and 'human scum'. Things went from bad to worse when UMNO lashed out at Indians and Chinese, calling them enemies of the State and promising to defend the Malay Muslim population against such subversives by means of the draconian ISA. At that time, the cult of keris

[9] was widely used to intimidate the non-Malays. To UMNO, the keris was a marker of Malay supremacy, a symbol of power, ownership and defence of the status quo. In Klang, that message of ethno-nationalist dominance was reinforced by erecting a Kris Monument in the town in 1985-a towering silver dagger on a massive plinth which was a public declaration of Malay-Muslim hegemony. It was an arrow to the heart of Mohan and all non-Malays. It said: 'non-Malays, know your place!' Its presence in Klang was intended to strike fear into the minds and hearts of those 'who do not belong'.

Fear invades men of every age and race and every walk of life. It is subtle and devastating, poisoning one's thinking and robbing one's inner peace. Fear creates victims and victims will not remain silent and subservient forever. After all, if you kick a dog every day, one day it will bite you. To Mohan and his socialist comrades, the Kris Monument was racism writ large; it was a blatant act of provocation that called for a response. A few days later, in the middle of the night, Mohan and a small band of his socialist comrades visited the Keris Monument and daubed it all over in red paint.

Not surprisingly, the defacement of the sacred symbol of UMNO was deemed an act of sacrilege and all hell broke loose. In the eyes of UMNO, the attack on the keris was tantamount to blasphemy. There were angry demonstrations and calls for retribution. The mufti in nearby Shah Alam said it was a plot by the Vatican and he called for the burning of bibles and the bombing of churches. However, the Prime Minister managed to quell the storm. He decreed that all churches and Mission schools in Selangor and KL were to be protected because he did not want Malaysia to be known as a police state (which it was) and he was apprehensive that any overt anti-Christian action might disrupt the flow of foreign money into the country. The twin pillars of UMNO were power and money. He also instructed the head of police in Klang to 'nab' the perpetrators of the outrage. It did not take the chief of police long to 'nab' the suspects – Mohan Pillai and a number of his socialist comrades. Mohan was duly arrested and interrogated, during which process he was beaten black and blue and repeatedly ordered to confess to the crime of defacing the keris. They searched his premises looking for red paint or spatters of paint on clothing but found nothing. Obviously, they were out to get Mohan with or without any material evidence. They were waiting for an opportunity to silence the PRSM even though it had already been disbanded. Nobody in Klang was surprised when Mohan suddenly disappeared. Under the ISA, he was arrested, accused of subversion and sent to the Kamunting Detention Camp.[10]

In Malaysia, the last place you want to be is in the Kamunting Detention Camp, outside the town of Taiping in Perak. For over 30 years, it was used by the government to detain, interrogate and rehabilitate persons arrested under the ISA. Kamunting was not a hell hole like the gulag in Russia. Most of the ISA detainees lived in communal cell blocks and were permitted to move within designated areas of the compound. They were allowed one visit a week from relatives and were entitled to receive fruit and reading material. They were encouraged to read, write or study and they could make and sell handicrafts. The food was bland and basic, served on a plastic tray. However, Kamunting was not exactly a holiday camp. Disruptive detainees were housed separately in punishment cells where they remained in solitary confinement and were allowed out of the cell only from 7am to 11am. They were not provided with a bed or mattress but slept on the cement floor. The cells had no light only an air vent. The camp was run by prison officers backed up by a reserve force of 60 riot police known as UKP. They were frequently used to quell disturbances by detainees who were handcuffed and so brutally beaten that they suffered from broken bones.

Initially, Mohan was in cell block T2B where he was abused and treated like a common criminal. A UKP officer interrogated him and having accused him of all sorts of dastardly deeds, demanded cigarettes. When Mohan replied that he had none, the officer called him a 'lying bastard' and punched his head against the wall. Then, two more guards spat in his face and called him 'an Indian cur'. He remined in T2B for almost a month, during which time he was regularly beaten but he refused to say whether he was involved in Keris Monument affair, which his accusers described as an act of subversion. His legal team in Klang made several attempts to appeal his sentence but all to no avail. The only concession was his release from solitary confinement to the communal cell block which he shared with two other Indian detainees and a very lively and intelligent Indonesian, Arif Zulkifli who was accused of spying for Indonesia during the Konfrontasi,[11] a charge which was a total fabrication. He swore that he was employed by the Java Spice Corporation to promote Indonesian spices in Sabah and Sarawak. He was known to all in the camp as Zul and he was treated with a measure of respect for two things. Firstly, he was a great story teller and he had no end of spicy tales about the Indonesian Sultanates such as the tale of the Sultan who married a mermaid,[12] tales of the various 'hantu'[13] that had to be appeased, and many tales of the beautiful but deadly vampire, the Pontianak[14] who preyed on male victims driven by lust. With Zul in full flow, his comrades enjoyed an endless stream of Indonesian folklore, punctuated by chants and age-old songs. Secondly, he was an expert on spices from his native Java and he received a regular supply of spices from his family, which greatly improved the taste of the bland food that was served daily in the camp. It was Zul who advised Mohan to trade in spices on his return to Klang. He convinced Mohan that spices were gold dust and he elaborated on the culinary and medicinal properties of cardamom, ginger, turmeric and tamarind.

Mohan's five-year detention sentence ended in June 1990. Since then, he has refused to discuss or write about his years of internment. He just wants to erase that horrific experience from his mind and get on with his life. On his return home, he was hardly recognisable. He was thin, gaunt and emaciated-a shadow of the man he once was. He obviously suffered severe physical and mental torture in captivity. His jet-black hair had greyed and he walked with a limp. However, he did not lose any of his burning desire for social justice and equality of esteem for all Malaysians. He still held utter contempt for the philistinism and corruption of the political establishment. Obviously, his aging parents were greatly relieved to have him back home. Their fruit business was booming and they decided that Mohan deserved a much-needed vacation in the land of their ancestors, Kerala.

Mohan's visit to Kerala transformed his life. Within days of his arrival in the Land of Spices, he met his future wife, Abby Bamai. It was a whirlwind romance in a land of surpassing natural beauty and gracious living. It was Abby who took Mohan on a tour of the spice plantations on the hills of the Western Ghats where the best spices in the world are cultivated. He was blown away by the massive plantations and the many spice stations that traded in cardamom, cloves, cinnamon, ginger, turmeric, nutmeg and tamarind. Everyone was full of admiration for one particular spice, the tamarind [15] which is widely used for flavouring in Asian cookery and in addition has valuable medicinal properties. For Indians, tamarind is the king of spices-the gold dust that Zul had often spoken of.

Back in Klang, Mohan and his newly married wife Abby decided that the old fruit shop needed a major makeover. It was extended with a fruit section on one side and spices on the other. The new emporium was named 'Mohan Spices and Herbals' dealing in all kinds of spices and medicinal herbs with therapeutic value. It became famous especially for the sticky brown spice called tamarind-the real thing imported directly from Kerala. It was so popular that Mohan became known across the Klang Valley as the 'Tamarind Man'. Very soon he became a very wealthy man and the local UMNO chiefs invited him to join their coalition. The devout socialist however declined to join the band of thieves, saying: 'You will never rehabilitate me in your image and likeness.'

ENDNOTES:

1   *Klang*: A large town that straddles the Klang River on the west coast of Malaysia. It was the former capital of Selangor. It has a large population of people of Indian origin and its main street is known as Little India. It is not the most beautiful town in the Klang Valley.

2   *makan*: food

3   *Deepavali*: The Hindu Festival of Lights

4   *PSRM*: Parti Socialis Rakyat Malaysia, the Malaysian Socialist Party, disbanded in 1974 due to massive state repression.

5   *Internal Security Act (ISA)*: A draconian Act that came into force 1960 to provide for the internal security of Malaysia following the armed insurgency conducted by Chin Peng and the Malayan Communist Party (MNLA). Persons suspected of being engaged in offences against the state were arrested and detained without trial at the Taiping Detention Camp. The Act was amended many times and its scope widened to include any person deemed to be a 'subversive' including trade unionists, labour activists, political activists, religious groups, academic bloggers etc. It was used a political weapon to stifle legitimate opposition and lawful dissent. The ISA was repealed in 2012. For a critique of the ISA see

Therese Lee, 'Malaysia and the Internal Security Act: The insecurity of human rights after September 11.' (Singapore Journal of Legal Studies, 2002: 56-72.)

6   *BN*: Barisan Nasional (National Front)-the ruling coalition of 14 component political parties, of which *UMNO*, (representing the Malays), MCA (representing the Chinese) and MIC (representing the Indians) are the largest. The BN/ UMNO coalition ruled Malaysia from Independence in 1957 to May 2018 when it was ousted by the new coalition called Pakatan Harapan, under Mahathir Mohamad, the former head of UMNO.

7   *Dean Johns*: A witty Australian journalist and blogger. His books and weekly columns for Malaysiakini.com are a rich source of socio-political commentary on the endemic corruption of the BN/UMNO regime. The reference here is to his collection of papers called 1MALAYSIA.CON, published by SIRD, Petaling Jaya, 2011.

8   *Straits Settlements*: The former British Crown colony along the strait of Malacca comprising the four trading posts of Penang, Malacca, Labuan and Singapore.

9   *Keris*: a dagger of different shapes and sizes, fundamentally a weapon denoting bloodletting, long esteemed as a sacred object with spiritual power among the elite of Javanese-Hindu society. It was adopted by Malay-Muslims as a maker of identity and ethno-nationalist culture and politics.

10   *Kamunting*: A town in Perak famous for its prison camp for detainees under the Internal Security Act. Also known as Malaysia's Gitmo.

11   *Konfrontasi*: The Indonesia-Malaysia confrontation (1963-66) stemming from Indonesia's opposition to the creation of the Federation of Malaysia in 1963 and control of the island of Borneo.

12   *The Sultan and the Mermaid Queen*: The famous Indonesian epic tale retold by Paul S. Sochaczewski. (2008: 74-91). Singapore: Editions Didier Millet.

13   *hantu*: ghosts

14   *Pontianak:* The dreaded vampire of Indonesian folklore who appeared young and beautiful in order to attract male victims.

15   *tamarind:* a sticky brown spice from the pod of the tamarind tree, long cultivated in Java and India. It is widely used as a flavouring in Asian cookery. It has known antioxidant and anti-inflammatory properties and it is especially good for reversing fatty liver disease. Origin: from Arabic *tamr hindi* 'Indian date'.

—-The end—-

POSTSCRIPT:
WRITING IN AND
ABOUT MALAYSIA

Malaysia is a great place for imagining the old colonial feel, due mainly to the classic tales of Somerset Maugham, Conrad's oriental novels and Anthony Burgess's 'Malayan Trilogy'. Everywhere, there are constant reminders of the colonial era, as seen in the architecture, street names, Mission schools and the many loan words from Malay and Chinese that add colour to Malaysian English. The following are some of the great books about the colonial period in Malaysia and Southeast Asia that will be familiar to many readers of my generation.

Henri Fauconnier (1931). *The Soul of Malaya*. Translated from the French by E. Sutton, E. Mathews, Marrot. This is both a documentary and social commentary on plantation life and European mores unravelling in the tropical heat. In 1906, Fauconnier opened his own rubber plantation at Rantau Panjang on the hills beyond the Selangor River.

Wm Somerset Maugham (1969). *Collected Short Stories. Vols. 1 – 4*. First published by Heinemann in 1969 and simultaneously in Singapore and Hong Kong for the expatriate and local school market. Of particular interest are the following:

Ah King; Six Stories. (1990). Heinemann & Bernhard Tauchnitz
Far Eastern Tales [Vintage Classics]. Singapore: Mandarin.

A Writer's Notebook (1949) [15 volumes in all]. London: W. Heinemann
The Casuarina Tree (1926). London: W. Heinemann

G. V. de Freitas (1985). *Maugham's Borneo Stories*. This collection was edited by de Freitas and contains many of Maugham's best stories, including 'The Outstation' and 'The Yellow Streak'. Published by Mandarin Paperbacks, Singapore.

Anthony Burgess (1981). *The Long Day Wanes: A Malayan Trilogy*. Penguin. Burgess set out to show how the sun had finally set on the British Empire in these three stories. Like Fauconnier, he actually lived and worked in Malaysia. He joined the British Colonial Service as a teacher at the Malay College in Kuala Kangar in Perak in 1935 but after a disagreement with the headmaster over accommodation he moved to the Malay Teachers' Training College at Kota Bharu in Kelantan.
Anthony Burgess (Ed.) (1969). *Maugham's Malaysian Stories*. Hong Kong: Heinemann
Anthony Burgess (1961). *Devil of a State*. London: Norton. In 1958 Burgess and his wife moved to Brunei and he took up a teaching post at SOAS College. He hated Brunei and wanted to write about it but for reasons of libel, he invented a country in East Africa which was named Naraka, meaning 'hell'. The novel, 'Devil of a State' is about Brunei.

Joseph Conrad (1895) is remembered in Malaysia for his oriental novels, *Almayer's Folly*, An *Outcast of the Islands* and *Lord Jim*. *Almayer's Folly*, published in 1895, is Joseph Conrad's first novel. It is about the misadventures of Kaspar Almayer, a young Dutch trader who is taken under the wing of the wily Captain Lingard.
An Outcast of the Islands Conrad's second novel is a tale of intrigue set in a trading post in Macassar. *Lord Jim,* published in 1900, is a powerful tale of a man in search of redemption. He ends up in self-enforced exile as a white trader in the remote outpost of Patusan, Borneo.
Graham Brash (1983). *Short Stories of the Far East*. Singapore: Graham Brash Publishing. This is a collection of 16 outstanding short stories by Joseph Conrad, Somerset Maugham, Pearl S. Buck and others.

Ralph P. Modder (2000). *There are no Chinamen in Singapore and other stories of British colonial days.* Singapore: Raffles.

Curse of the Pontianak. (2004) Singapore: Horizon Books.

The Red Cheongsam and other tales of Malaya and Singapore. (2006). A collection of 31 stories giving glimpses of life in the colonial era in Malaya and Singapore. Singapore: Horizon Books.

A Getai Singer's Love Affair with a Ghost and other true 'Hungry Ghost' Stories. (2007). Singapore: Horizon Books.

Modder is a professional journalist with several other collections of short stories. He was born in Malaysia but lives in Singapore where he has been a journalist with the 'Straits Times'. He has also written about the fall of Singapore in *The Passionate Islanders: A Factual Story, Singapore at War 1941-42.* Singapore: Horizon Books (2010).

Reginald Hugh Hickling (1957). *Festival of Hungry Ghosts.* Petaling Jaya: Pelanduk Publications.

Crimson Sun over Borneo: a novel. (1968) Petaling Jaya: Pelanduk Publications.

A Prince of Borneo. (1985) Singapore: Graham Brash.

The Dog Satyricon. (1994) Pedaling Jaya: Pelanduk Publications. This is a mixture of truth and fantasy that the author claims to have gleaned from the mouths of fellow club members of the Royal Selangor Club (The Dog of the title), allegedly while imbibing on the Club's verandah. *Memoir of a Wayward Lawyer.* (2000) Bangi: Universiti Kabangsan Malaysia.

Hickling, known in Malaysia as Hugh Hickling, was a British lawyer, colonial civil servant, law academic and author. In 1950, he was posted to Sarawak, then a British colony where, as he puts it, he 'cheerfully assisted in the dissolution of the Empire.' In Malaysia, he is remembered for something other than his novels. He helped to frame the Constitution and he drafted the controversial Internal Security Act (1960) but he did not expect the law to be used against political opponents.

Mahbob Abdullah (2003). *Planter's Tales: A Plantation Manager's Stories.* Malaysia: ICP Services. Mahbob Abdullah chose planting as a career in the early 60s and he spent his working life on plantations in Perak and abroad. His plantation tales, 60 in all, cover real events and experiences on the plantations.

Planter Upriver. (2009). Kuala Lumpur: Silverfish Books.

Catherine Lim: Born in Malaysia, now living in Singapore, Lim is one of the most prolific writers in Southeast Asia. She has published nine collections of short stories. See *The Best of Catherine Lim*. Heinemann Asia, Singapore, 1993. She has published five novels including the much admired *Following the Wrong God Home*. (2001) London: Orion.

Leslie Davidson (2007). *East of Kinabalu: Tales from the Borneo Jungle.* ISP Publications. Davidson was responsible for bringing oil palm to Sabah. He also introduced the pollinating weevil. The redoubtable Scotsman began his oil palm mission on an estate in Kluang, Johor in 1951. Kluang was one of the worst black spots of the Emergency and on his first day on the estate his manager issued him with a Winchester carbine, an automatic pistol and an armoured car. Later he moved to Cameroon in Africa and in 1960 he made his way to Sabah where he set up the Tungul Palm oil Plantation up the Labuk River from Sandakan.

Much of the new writing is exceptionally good. There are several very good novelists and short story writers in Malaysia, including the following:

Tan Twan Eng (2012). *The Garden of Evening Mists.* Myrmidon Books.

Tan Twan Eng (2009). *The Gift of Rain.* Hachette Books

Tash Aw (2011). *The Harmony Silk Factory.* Harper Collins.

Heidi Munan (2005). *Malayan Stories.* Kuala Lumpur: Utusan Publications.

Lee Su Kim (2011). *Kebaya Tales.* Shah Alam: Marshall Cavendish (Malaysia).

Shaari Isa (2010). *Did It Really Happen.* Petaling Jaya: MPH Group Publishing.

Chua Kok Yee (2010). *Without Anchovies.* Kuala Lumpur: Silverfish Books.

Khoo Khong Kor (2011). *The Four-sided Tower.* Subang Jaya: Pelanduk Publications

Dian Zaman (2012). *King of the Sea.* Kuala Lumpur: Silverfish Books.

Non-fiction:

As regards non-fiction, it is beyond the scope of this review to offer a comprehensive listing. Instead, I simply include a few of my favourite works in random order.

Agnes Newton Keith (1939). *Land Below the Wind.* (Reprint ed.1952) Michael Joseph.

Danny Lim (2008). *The Malaysian Book of the Undead.* Kuala Lumpur: Mata Hari Books.

Redmond O'Hanlon (1984). *Into the Heart of Borneo.* Penguin, New ed. 2005.

C. H. Gallop ('Pengembara') (2008). *Wanderer in Malaysian Borneo.* Shah Alam: Marshall Cavendish (Malaysia).

Peter Eaton (2010). *Borneo and Beyond.* Subang Jaya: Pelanduk.

R. H. W. Reece (1982). *The Name of Brooke: The end of White Rajah rule in Sarawak.* Kuala Lumpur: Oxford University Press.

F. Spencer Chapman. (1945). *The Jungle is Neutral.* London: Chatto & Windus.

N. Barbar (1971). *War of the Running Dogs.* London: Collins.

S. Francis (1990). *Borneo in History.* (A catalogue of books in the Borneo Collection of the library of the University of Brunei). Brunei University Library.

Anthony Milner (2010). *The Malays.* John Wiley & Sons.

Brett Atkinson et al. (2019). *Lonely Planet Best of Malaysia and Singapore.* Lonely Planet, UK.

Jim Baker (2020). *Crossroads: A Popular History of Malaysia and Singapore.* (4th ed.) Marshall Cavendish.

ACKNOWLEDGEMENTS

A number of people have helped me, in one way or another, in writing the stories in *Tall Tales of Malaysia*. In particular, I appreciate the comments and feedback received from the following: Loo Seng Piew (Penang), Alan Chamberlain (New South Wales) and David Bourke (Dublin).

For general knowledge on Malaysia, I am grateful to W. Moore & G. Cubitt (2000). *This is Malaysia*. London: New Holland Publishers.

I am especially grateful for information about Malaysia in three books which were constantly on my desk during the writing of Tall *Tales*. They are:

Farish A. Noor (2009*)*. *What Your Teacher Didn't Tell You*. Kuala Lumpur: Mata Hari.

Danny Lim (2008). *The Malaysian Book of the Undead*. Kuala Lumpur: Mata Hari.

Peter Anderson (1995). *Discover Borneo-Sarawak: a travel guide*. Petaling Jaya: Photo Images & Design, Sdn Bhd.

Any factual errors or infelicities in the stories are entirely mine. The stories are entirely fictional and belong to the category of modern lore.

I wish to thank my editor and the production team at AuthorHouse UK for their support and technical assistance in preparing my text for publication.

By the same author:

Under The Alien Sky (2010). An oriental novel

Footprints in the Mind (2010). Short stories

Two Plays for Tuppence (2016). Two plays written for television

Confessions of an Alien (2016). A novel

Requiem for the Republic (2021). Critical essays

Stories from Irish History (2021). Short stories.